Camp Club Girls

Kate's
Philadelphia Frenzy

Published by Barbour Publishing, Inc., P.O. Box 719, Uhrichsville, Ohio 44683, www.barbourbooks.com

Our mission is to publish and distribute inspirational products offering exceptional value and biblical encouragement to the masses.

 Member of the
Evangelical Christian
Publishers Association

Printed in the United States of America.

Dickinson Press, Inc.; Grand Rapids, MI; April 2010; D10002265

Camp Club Girls

Kate's
Philadelphia Frenzy

Janice Hanna

BARBOUR
PUBLISHING

Calling All Supersleuths!

Cr-r-rack! The Philadelphia Phillies baseball player hit the ball with his bat and the noise split the air in the stadium. The dirty white orb soared over the field at lightning speed, heading right for the stands. Kate Oliver watched it, her heart thumping wildly as it sailed in her direction.

All around her the fans hollered, "Catch it, catch it!" at the top of their lungs.

Catch it?

"Oh no! You don't understand! I don't know *anything* about baseball!" Kate murmured. The girl in front of her ducked, and Kate stuck her hand up in the air, knowing she couldn't possibly catch a baseball, especially not one moving this fast! She started sweating as it flew closer, closer, closer!

With a *ka-thump*, it smacked against her open palm. "Owie!" Man, did it hurt! She looked down at the ball, shocked. Shaking like a leaf, Kate whispered, "I did it! I really did it! I caught the ball!"

All around her the fans cheered. The players on the field clapped their hands as they looked her way. Kate stood up, held the ball in the air, and bowed as the stadium roared, "Go, Kate! Go, Kate! Go, Kate!"

Then—quite suddenly—she woke up.

"What a dream!" Kate said with a groan. "I couldn't catch a baseball if someone paid me a million dollars!"

She trembled as she thought about the ball flying toward her. Why would she dream about baseball when she'd never even been to a game before?

From the corner of the room she heard a strange *ka-thunk, ka-thunk, ka-thunk*. Odd. The same sound as in the dream. Kate squinted her eyes in the summer morning light to see Biscuit, her dog, playing with a baseball. He rolled it with his nose across the hardwood floor until it hit the wall. Then he grabbed it in his mouth and began to chew on it. A few seconds later, he rolled it across the floor till it hit the wall once again. *Ka-thunk!*

"Oh no!" Kate jumped out of bed and grabbed the gooey, chewed-up ball. "Not the ball Andrew's dad signed for me!"

Biscuit whimpered and tucked his tail between his legs. "Go ahead and apologize, you nutty dog!" Kate said. "It won't do you any good. This ball is worth a lot of money!" She held up the slobbery ball and sighed as she saw the chew marks. "Well, it *was* worth a lot of money."

Clutching the ball, she suddenly realized why she must've dreamed about baseball. *Oh, that's right! I have a mystery to solve. . .a very important one!* But she couldn't do it alone. No, she needed help from one of the Camp Club girls!

Kate put on her glasses then tapped a button on the phone beside her bed and said, "Sydney."

The phone automatically dialed the number and Kate heard it ring. "Answer the phone, Sydney! C'mon, answer. . .please!" she coaxed.

"H—hello?"

"Sydney!" Kate squealed. "This is Kate. I'm *so* glad you're awake."

"Awake?" Sydney sounded groggy. She groaned and said, "Kate, it's seven in the morning. . .on a *Saturday*. I'm *not* awake yet. Can you call back later?"

"No, please don't hang up! I need you," Kate said. "It's really important."

The tone of Sydney's voice changed. "What's happened? Are you hurt? Is it one of the other girls? Who's in trouble? What's happened?"

Kate couldn't help but laugh. "Nothing's happened to me or any of the other Camp Club Girls. We're all fine. But something's going on here in Philly—something really big—and I need your help. I sent you an e-mail a couple of days ago, but you didn't answer. Didn't you get it?"

"I've been at sports camp, remember?" Sydney said. "I

sent you a text message last week."

"Oh yeah. I forgot. Sorry." Kate started to explain why she called, but just then Biscuit came to the edge of the bed and started whimpering. *Ar-ooo! Ar-ooo!*

Kate groaned. "Hang on, Sydney. Biscuit won't stop crying till I put him on the bed. He's so spoiled."

"Okay." Sydney yawned loudly. "But you're the one who spoils him. You always have. . .ever since that first day when we found him at camp."

"I know, I know. I can't help myself." Kate reached down and lifted Biscuit—the wonder dog—onto the bed, and he gave her face a couple of slobbery kisses. "Eew, stinky breath! Gross!"

Not that she really minded. She'd loved him from that first day when the Camp Club Girls found him on the golf course. Slobbery kisses or not! Chewed-up baseballs or not!

He gave her one more kiss and almost knocked off her glasses. She pushed them back up with her index finger and turned to the dog using her sternest voice. "Down, boy!" He rolled over onto his back, ready for a tummy rub. "No, silly. I'll do that later, if you let me talk on the phone!"

He finally curled up at her side and she went back to talking to Sydney. "Are you still there?"

"Yes, but what were you saying?" Sydney asked with another yawn. " 'Cause if this can wait, I want to go back to sleep. I'm tired. They really worked us out at sports camp.

We ran four miles every morning and played team sports for the rest of the day. Every muscle in my body hurts."

"I'm sorry, but please don't hang up yet." Kate didn't mean to sound so firm, but she couldn't help it. "That's why I'm calling you, because you're the biggest sports nut in the Camp Club Girls."

"Hey, are you calling me *big*?" Sydney pretended to sound offended.

"No, silly."

"You're calling me a nut?"

"No." Kate laughed. "I meant sports *fan*. I need a friend who knows something about baseball."

"Well, why didn't you say so? I *love* baseball." Sydney, now sounding completely awake, began to talk about some of her favorite players and some of her all-time favorite games. None of it made a lick of sense to Kate, who cared nothing about baseball or any other sport.

Kate didn't want to interrupt her, but she had no choice. "Sydney, I'm sure those people are all great, but I need to tell you about something big that's happening here in Philadelphia."

"What?"

"Do you know Tony Smith? The Phillies shortstop?"

"Are you kidding? Of course!" Sydney squealed. "Who doesn't? Do you know how many awards that guy has won? He's a great player. There's such a cool story about how he came to play for the Phillies. He's a free agent, you know. I read all about it online a few months ago."

"Yes, but have you read anything in the past couple days?" Kate asked. " 'Cause now people on the Web are posting stories, saying he's not happy playing for the Phillies. They're calling him all sorts of names and saying he wants to play for another team."

"No way." Sydney gasped. "That's too bad. I thought he liked Philadelphia. I guess I need to catch up on my reading."

"No, that's just it. He *does* like it here." Kate sighed. "Look, I don't really know that much about baseball. Or basketball. Or football. Or any kind of sports, really. But Tony's son, Andrew, is my friend. He says the stories aren't true, that someone started rumors just to hurt his dad."

"Are you serious?" Sydney's voice grew more excited. "Wait. . .you know the son of a pro baseball player? Can you get his father's autograph? Tell him you have a friend in DC who wants a signed poster. If he says no, tell him I ran track and field in the Junior Olympics. That should do it. He can autograph it to Sydney Lincoln, the future Olympian."

"Slow down, slow down!" Kate laughed. "We can talk about autographs later. You're not letting me finish the story. Andrew says someone's out to get his dad by putting lies on the Web. They're making Tony look really bad. Some of the players and fans are mad at him over something that's not even true. So Andrew asked me to help him figure out who's trying to frame his dad, but I need your help."

"Sydney Lincoln, baseball fan, at your service. Just tell me what to do."

Kate giggled. "Well, you can pray, of course. But there's something else, too. Can you come to Philly and stay with me for a couple weeks till we get to the bottom of this? We've got to stop whoever is setting up Mr. Smith."

"Wait, what do you mean? Come to your house? Like, a vacation?"

"Sure, why not? You'll be here for my birthday. It's on the Fourth of July, you know."

"Oh, that's right! I remember. And right in the middle of baseball season. Talk about perfect timing!"

"Better than you think! Andrew and his dad gave me tickets for the Tuesday night game. We're going to sit just behind the dugout."

"No way!"

"Yep." Kate grew more excited as she spoke. "My mom will call your mother today to ask her if you can come. You can take the train from DC."

"To Philadelphia? Woo-hoo!" Sydney squealed. "Ooh! Puh-*leeze* pray my mom says yes. I want to come so much! Can you imagine how exciting this is going to be? Two supersleuths working together. . .again!" After a moment's pause, she asked, "Have you let the other Camp Club Girls know yet?"

"No. We'll e-mail them," Kate responded. "But I need you on site, Sydney, because you know about baseball. I really don't know anything. To me, those guys in uniform just look like they're running around. The whole thing is kind of, well, boring."

Sydney laughed. "There's more to it than running in circles—and it's not boring—but you can count on me to help you figure things out. And by the end of this, you'll know a lot about baseball, I promise. Maybe I'll even turn you into a fan!"

"Now that would really be something!" Just then Kate heard a knock on her door. She hollered, "Come in!" then whispered, "Hang on a minute, Sydney."

Her mother popped her head in the door. "G'morning, sunshine! Is that Sydney? Did you ask her if she wants to come visit?"

Kate nodded and smiled. "Yes!"

"Great! I'll call her mother after breakfast and see if she'll bring her to Philly on tomorrow's train. How does that sound?"

"Delicious!" Kate shouted. A wonderful aroma filled the room. Kate closed her eyes and drew in a deep breath. "Ooh, speaking of delicious, is that bacon I smell cooking downstairs?"

"Yes. I'm making pancakes and scrambled eggs, too."
Her mom winked. "Come down as soon as you're done
with your call." She closed the door.

"Mmm." Kate turned her attention back to Sydney.
"Sydney, I've gotta go. Breakfast calls. But talk to your mom
quick, before my mother calls her, okay? That way she's
prepared. We want her to have time to think about it. Oh,
and Sydney?"

"Yes?"

"Thanks. I *really* need you."

"Aw, you're welcome." Sydney giggled. "Just pray my
mom says yes, okay?"

"Okay. I'm praying." Kate hung up the phone and bowed
her head to pray. If she ever needed help from above. . .it
was now!

CHAPTER 2

Gadgets and Gizmos

After praying, Kate bounded down the stairs with Biscuit on her heels. He yapped, yapped, yapped the whole way! What a silly little dog!

She stopped to look in the large round mirror that hung on the stairway wall. Her shoulder-length blond hair needed to be combed, and her glasses were smudged and crooked again. Oh well. No one cared, right? She couldn't be a supersleuth and have perfect hair at the same time, could she? Oh, but if only she could do something about those freckles!

As soon as she got to the bottom floor, Kate ran smack-dab into Robby, the robo-vac. As always, Biscuit started barking at the funny little vacuum cleaner that kept the floor clean.

Ruff, ruff! Ruff, ruff! Biscuit took several steps backward but never stopped barking.

"Stop it, Biscuit! I've told you a hundred times. . .Robby won't hurt you."

"That's right," her mother called out from the kitchen. "And besides, Robby's doing us a favor, picking up all of the dog hair that Biscuit sheds."

The dog reached out his paw and tried to tap the vacuum cleaner. It turned around and went the other way. Kate giggled. "See? You'll never be friends if you keep hurting his feelings!"

She went into the kitchen and practically drooled when she saw the yummy food. Bacon sizzled on the stove and a skillet filled with fluffy yellow eggs looked delicious. To the side of the stove she saw a big stack of pancakes. And the table was set with their nicest dishes, the ones mom only used on very special occasions. *Something big must be happening.* Kate the supersleuth would find out what it was. . .pronto!

"Mom, what's up?"

"Your dad got a patent for one of his projects," her mother said with a smile. "Remember that robotic security system he's been working on in the basement?"

"SWAT-bot?" Kate's eyes widened. "The little robot with the police uniform? Really? That's so cool!"

"Yes, so we're celebrating in style." Her mom lowered her voice. "Be sure to tell him how proud you are, okay, honey?"

"Oh, I am proud!" Kate wanted to be just like her dad when she grew up.

"Good girl." Her mother smiled. "After breakfast I'll call

Sydney's mom. I know how much you need your friend's help right now."

"I really do, Mom. She knows everything there is to know about baseball. And I think she and Andrew will be good friends."

"Andrew's a great kid," her mother said. "And I'm so happy the Smiths have been coming to church. I've enjoyed getting to know his mom."

"And Andrew loves it, too," Kate said. "But he's been so upset over this thing with his dad that I'm afraid he'll stop coming. Some of the kids in our class at church are saying mean things. They think his dad's a traitor to the team, and Andrew's really upset. That's why I want to help him."

"That's my girl," Kate's dad said, entering the room. "Always helping others."

Kate rushed to her father and hugged him. "G'morning, Dad!"

"Good morning, pumpkin. What's this about Andrew's feelings getting hurt?"

"People are spreading untrue stories about his dad," she explained.

"Ah. So the rumor mill is at work?"

"Rumor mill?" Kate asked. "What's that?"

"Oh, it's just an expression," he explained. "When lots of people are talking about someone behind his back, it's called a rumor mill."

"The Bible is pretty clear about gossiping," Kate's mother said as she put the food on the table. "The Lord doesn't like it. . .at all! People get hurt once the rumor mill gets going, just like Andrew and his dad. And his mom, too."

Kate sighed. "I want to help make them feel better."

"That's my girl." Her father kissed her on the forehead and then looked around. "Where's Dex?"

"I thought I heard him moving around in his room earlier." Kate's mother looked around.

"I'll bet he's still asleep," Kate said. Her little brother often slept in late on Saturdays.

"No, I'm not."

They all turned as they heard his voice. Dexter entered the room in his pajamas with his hair sticking up all over his head. Kate couldn't help but laugh at the funny blond spikes. He looked like a martian.

Dex sat down and their father prayed over the food. Kate loved to hear her father pray. It always made her feel so good inside.

As they all ate yummy warm pancakes drizzled with maple syrup, he started talking about SWAT-bot.

"I'm so excited about the new patent," Kate's dad said with a grin. "This will open so many doors for my inventions. And SWAT-bot will be featured in a prominent scientific magazine, too. That's quite an honor."

"I'm so proud of you, Dad," Kate said when he finished.

"This is the neatest thing that's happened to our family in ages!"

"It is pretty cool," he admitted.

"Will you be on the news?" she asked.

"Oh, I don't think so, honey. Getting a patent isn't like being a big sports star or something."

"Well, it should be!" She paused and then said, "Andrew's dad is famous, and now my dad is, too!" She stuffed more pancakes into her mouth, adding a quiet, "Mmm!"

Her father laughed. "Well, I don't know about being famous. I'd just as soon *not* be! There's a lot of pressure on people like Tony Smith to perform well. Not a lot of people even know what I do, so if I make a mistake, people are less likely to notice."

"Speaking of sports, is it still okay if Sydney and I go to the game with Andrew and his mom on Tuesday night?" Kate asked.

"I think so," her mother said. "I'll talk to Andrew's mother and make sure she's comfortable taking two preteen girls. If she's fine with it, I'm fine with it."

"Cool! Andrew's whole family is going to love Sydney. She knows everything about baseball. I know nothing." Kate couldn't help but sigh. "But maybe I'll learn something while I'm there."

"I suppose I should have taught you more about sports," her father said, shaking his head. "Maybe I should've taken you to a few Phillies games or watched football with you on television. I've just always been more interested in technology. Sorry, kiddo."

"Who needs sports anyway?" Kate giggled. "Seriously, I love the gadgets and gizmos you bring home from work, Dad. You know how crazy I am about electronics. And I don't miss being involved in sports at all. . .honest."

She grinned and took another bite of food.

"Me either, Dad," Dexter agreed, wrinkling his nose. "I'd rather help you build things. Who needs baseballs and footballs and stuff?"

"Well, the apple doesn't fall far from the tree, does it?" Their father winked.

Kate looked at him curiously. *Apple? Tree?*

"He means you kids are just like he is," her mother said. "Like father, like daughter." Dexter frowned and their mother added, "And like father, like son!"

Kate laughed and asked her mother for another pancake. With so much work to do, she needed food to keep up her strength! Besides, the pancakes were terrific!

After breakfast, Kate pleaded, "Can you call Sydney's mom and ask if she can come? Now? Now, Mom?"

"All right, all right." Her mother rose from the table and grabbed her cell phone. "What's the number, again?"

Sydney jotted down her friend's telephone number on a napkin.

"Here you go, Mom. And please, please, please do your best convincing job! I really hope her mom says yes!"

Dexter headed off to play with a tiny electronic car, and minutes later, Kate's mother was talking with Sydney's mom on the phone. Kate could tell that Mrs. Lincoln liked the idea by the smile on her mom's face.

Kate hated to interrupt, but she had to know! "Can she come?" she whispered.

Her mother nodded and winked at her.

Kate squealed. "Tell her 'Thank you! Thank you!' " She jumped up and down; then she waited until her mother and Mrs. Lincoln worked out the details. After they ended the call, she asked, "When is Sydney coming?"

"Tomorrow afternoon. We'll pick her up at four o'clock at the train station. Now, before she gets here, you need to get upstairs and pick up that messy room, young lady. You can't have a guest with all of that clutter everywhere."

"Okay."

Kate went running up the stairs with Biscuit following behind. She looked at her messy room and sighed. "Where should I start?" She didn't mean to be a slob, but with so many things to keep up with, how could she be tidy?

Kate spent a few minutes tidying up. Then she got distracted, looking at the hope chest at the foot of her bed. It had belonged to her grandmother, and Kate stored her gadgets and gizmos in it. Her dad had carved the words

KATE'S GADGETS into the lid. She ran her finger along the words and smiled. How fun, to have a special place to keep all of her goodies!

She opened the lid and glanced inside, smiling when she saw the familiar items. Kate picked up the tiny black digital recorder, checking to make sure the batteries were good. She snapped it on and recorded a few words, then said, "Perfect!"

Next she found her teensy-tiny digital camera. She checked the memory card to make sure she had plenty of room for more pictures. Looked like she was in good shape there, too! "Great!"

Kate picked up something that looked like an ink pen. It was really a text reader. You could run it along words in a book and it would record them. She tested it by running it along the words in her Bible. Right away it recorded one of her favorite verses, Philippians 4:13: *I can do all things through Christ who strengthens me.* "Cool."

Thanks, Lord! I really needed that reminder. You're the One in charge of this case anyway, and I know You already have all the answers!

Next Kate reached for her MP3 player. It would certainly come in handy over the next couple of weeks.

So would the next gadget she pulled out. Kate stared at the computerized wristwatch her father had given her just a few days earlier. One of his students had invented it, and soon it would be sold in stores. She could hardly believe it was possible to check her e-mail or browse the Web on a wristwatch, but she had already tried it out and knew it worked! How exciting! Surely no one else her age had a watch like that!

Finally, Kate pulled out a pair of mirrored sunglasses, smiling as she put them on. "Yep. You really can see what's going on behind you when you're wearing these. Cool."

She spent the next half hour organizing the chest. Once she had everything in place, she closed the lid tightly, thinking about all of the treasures her dad had given her over the past few years. They would all come in handy after Sydney arrived and they got to work. In the meantime, she needed to get to work cleaning! One of her favorite Camp Club Girls would be here soon. What exciting adventures were ahead!

Inspector Gadet

"Hurry, hurry, hurry!" Kate bounced up and down, waiting for Sydney's train to arrive from DC. She glanced at the clock: 4:05. "They're late, Mom!"

"Only by a couple of minutes," her mother said. "Be patient, Kate!"

"But we have work to do!"

Minutes later, Kate heard a familiar voice. She looked up as Sydney rushed her way. Dozens of dark braids bounced around Sydney's head as she ran. Man! Was she ever fast!

Kate let out a squeal. "Oh, you're taller than last time!"

"Yes. I've grown two inches this year," Sydney announced, brushing a braid out of her face. She flashed a broad smile and her white teeth looked even whiter against her beautiful dark skin. "What about you?"

Kate sighed and slumped her shoulders. "No. Sometimes I wonder if I'm ever going to grow."

"It'll happen." Sydney laughed. "And if it makes you feel

any better, your freckles have grown since the last time I saw you."

Kate groaned. "They're always like this in the summertime. Wish they would just disappear!" She frowned just thinking about it. Why couldn't she be normal. . .like the other Camp Club Girls? Why did she have to be so. . .different?

"Aw, I think you look great!" Sydney said, interrupting her thoughts.

"Thanks." Maybe different wasn't so bad after all.

Just then a beautiful woman who looked a lot like Sydney rounded the corner, gasping for breath. "Sydney, you're too fast for me! I can't keep up!"

"Sorry, Mom!" Sydney giggled. "I've been running track for so long, I sometimes forget others aren't as fast."

"You must be Mrs. Lincoln!" Kate rushed to the woman and surprised her with a big hug. "Thank you, thank you for letting Sydney come! I'm so excited."

"Well, you're welcome. And. . .I can tell you're excited!"

"When do you have to catch the train back to DC?" Kate's mother asked Mrs. Lincoln. "Do you have time to come to our house for dinner?"

"No, I'm afraid I have to get right back. The train returns in twenty minutes, in fact. But that's really for the best. I have to be at work in the morning."

"We're so grateful you've brought Sydney to stay with

us," Kate's mother said. "We'll be in touch. And you have my number if you need anything."

"Thank you so much for inviting her. I'm sure she's going to have the time of her life!"

"I always have fun with Kate!" Sydney said.

Sydney and her mother said their good-byes, and then Mrs. Lincoln headed off on her way to catch the train back to DC.

The girls talked all the way back to the house. In fact, they arrived home in no time at all. Kate's mother fixed big, thick, juicy cheeseburgers and crispy fries for dinner— Kate's favorite. She ate not just one cheeseburger, but two. And she loaded up on fries, even asking for seconds.

"You sure can pack away a lot of food for such a tiny thing," Sydney said with a smile.

Kate shrugged. "I love burgers and fries."

"I'm trying to eat healthier," Sydney explained. "Especially since I'm involved in so many sports. Got to stay in tip-top shape."

"Hmm." Kate didn't comment. Maybe some people were meant to be in tip-top shape and others were not.

Biscuit began to whimper at her feet. She tore off a teensy-tiny piece of her hamburger and slipped it under the table.

"I saw that," her mother said. "Biscuit doesn't need table scraps. He has his own food."

"I know. Sorry," Kate said.

"Remember that first day we found Biscuit. . .at camp?" Sydney asked.

"How could I forget? He was so hungry—and so scraggly looking." Kate sighed. "I guess that's why I spoil him now. He had such a hard life before coming to live here."

"There's no harm in a little spoiling," her mother said with a wink. "Just not too much. Oh, and by the way, would you like to know what we're having for dessert?" When the girls nodded, she said, "Ice cream sundaes."

"Woo-hoo!" Kate added an extra scoop of ice cream to hers and poured on extra syrup. Then she put a huge dollop of whipped cream on top. It tasted like heaven! When she finished, she thought about asking for another sundae but decided not to. The girls would have plenty of time to eat later. Right now, they had a case to solve!

After dessert, Andrew stopped by. He took one look at Sydney and grinned with that crooked grin of his and said, "Wow, you're taller than I am."

"Yeah, maybe a little." Sydney shrugged. "But how old are you?" She gave him a curious look. "I'll bet I'm older."

"I'm eleven." He looked a little embarrassed.

"Well, I'm thirteen," Sydney explained. "So that explains it. But I am tall, even for my age." She sighed. "To be honest, I don't like being the tallest in my class. When I was younger I always had to stand in the back row in class pictures. I just wanted to be the little shrimp in the class like Kate here."

"Hey!" Kate pretended to be upset. "I'm no shrimp. Why do you keep talking about how short I am?"

"You're not short," her mother called out from the kitchen. "You're petite. Like me. That's a good thing."

"Yeah, I'm petite. That's a good thing," Kate repeated.

They all laughed, but inside she wondered if she would ever grow.

Andrew turned to Sydney with his arms crossed at his chest. "So Kate tells me you're a baseball fan. Have you ever played?"

"Yep. Played softball last year. And I'm a golf fan, and a football fan, and a track and field fan." Sydney grinned. "I love sports. Can you tell?"

"I can. And I love sports, too. Usually." A worried look came into Andrew's eyes. "Did Kate tell you about what's going on with my dad? All the terrible things people are saying?"

"Yes, and that really stinks! I think your dad is a great player, and he obviously loves his team. So we need to get busy trying to figure out who's trying to frame him."

"Yeah, but I don't know how we're going to do that. I don't even know where to start. I've never solved a crime before. Or cracked a case. Or whatever you call it."

"Just leave it to the Camp Club Girls!" Sydney said. "We're supersleuths."

"Supersleuths?" Andrew looked confused.

"Sure." Kate giggled. "Like Nancy Drew."

"Nancy *who*?" he asked, his brow wrinkling in confusion.

"Nancy *Drew*. . .oh, never mind." Kate slapped herself on the forehead. "You just have to trust us. We've solved a mystery or two before this one. That's why I called Sydney for her help."

"You're in good hands, in other words," Sydney said with a smile. She turned to Kate with a sparkle in her eye. "Kate, did you ever show Andrew all of your crime-solving gadgets?"

"Ooh! Good idea," Kate said.

"I've heard her talk about them, but I've never seen them," Andrew said.

"My dad teaches robotics at Penn State, and he's always bringing home the coolest stuff," Kate explained. "You wouldn't believe it. And here's the best part—there's always something new coming out, so I get his old stuff. Only, it's not old to me. It's really neat. And I've learned so much. I'm going to start inventing things like my dad. . .soon. We're already working on a top secret project."

She clamped her hand over her mouth, realizing she'd said too much. It wouldn't be top secret if she told people.

"Trust me when I say she's got *so* many amazing electronics," Sydney said. "When we were at camp, she showed us things we'd never seen before."

"Oh, I have a lot more stuff since Discovery Lake Camp," Kate explained. "So hang on. I'll be right back." She ran upstairs and grabbed several items out of her gadget chest. *Ooh, Andrew's going to love all of this!*

She came back downstairs a few minutes later, nearly dropping the armload of stuff. She could hardly wait to show them her gadgets.

"Wow." Andrew looked at her arms with wide eyes. "That's a lot!"

"My dad is always bringing home more. You think this is a lot—one day I'll take you down to his workroom in the basement and show you all the good stuff. It's like an electronics store down there, only better." She described several of the neatest things her dad had worked on. By the time she finished, Andrew and Sydney were staring at her with their mouths open.

"Your dad is amazing!" Sydney said.

"You are, too." Andrew still looked surprised by all of the things in her arms.

She put the items on the dining room table and they gathered around. One by one, she told Andrew about her goodies.

"This is a great digital recorder. It's different from most of the ones you can buy in stores because it's so tiny. And here's a pen that actually records text."

"Records text?" Andrew looked shocked.

"Yes. Watch." She ran it along the headline in the newspaper and it recorded the words TROUBLE IN THE PHILLIES CAMP.

"Hmm. Maybe we'd better save that one for later." She paused, examining the pile of electronics.

She reached for the bright red slimline cell phone. "I ended up with dad's cell phone when he got his new one. It has a GPS navigational system on it. And it's got a great camera and can even do video clips. Best of all, the cell phone is linked to our family's laptop, so I can send and receive files. My MP3 player is synced, too. Everything is connected. It's way better than an iPhone or any of the commercial phones. My dad showed me how to do all of that. And wait till you see this wristwatch." She pulled it out and Sydney and Andrew looked at it with curious expressions.

"I can't believe you're only eleven." Sydney shook her head. "You're just so. . .smart! You could be a professor or something. Or a scientist, even. Have you ever thought about that?"

"Sure, I think about it all the time," she said. "But you really don't need to build my ego! My little brother, Dexter, is almost nine and he already knows how to do most of this, too." Kate shrugged as she thought about it. "I guess our parents just taught us lots of different stuff from other kids. We're kind of like that family in *Honey, I Shrunk the*

Kids. Only, of course, our dad never shrunk us or anything like that. But he does have some cool inventions, just like the man in the movie."

"Well, I think your whole family is cool." Sydney picked up the cell phone and tossed it from one hand to another, like a baseball. After a couple of nervous looks from Kate, she put it back down. "I know!" Sydney squealed. "I'm going to start calling you Inspector Gadget because of all these gadgets and gizmos you own. I can't wait to tell the other girls."

"Inspector Gadget?" Kate laughed. "That's a good one."

"It fits you," Andrew said, looking at the digital recorder.

"Look at this," Kate said, holding up a tiny penlike device. "It's a translator, shaped like an ink pen."

"A translator?" Sydney asked. "What would you need that for?"

"Well, say you're in a situation where you find a clue, but it's written in a different language," Kate explained. "All you do is run the pen along the words, and then it translates the words into English so you can understand them."

"Wow, I guess that might come in handy," Sydney said.

"I came up with this one myself," she said, holding up a dog collar.

"Just looks like a regular collar," Sydney said. "Is it Biscuit's?"

"Yes," Kate explained, "but it's not an ordinary collar. It has a tiny built-in microphone that transmits to this receiver." She held up the tiny black receiver and smiled. "So let's say I send Biscuit over to a suspect and I want to hear something he or she is saying. I can hear every word through the microphone."

"That's pretty impressive," Andrew said. "So you girls use Biscuit to help you solve your cases, too?"

"Sometimes," Kate said. "Like that first mystery we solved at Discovery Lake Camp. He was a big help to us back then!"

"What else do you have?" Sydney asked, leaning down to look at the items.

"Hmm." Kate glanced at each one, finally pulling out a tiny metal clip. "This is a money clip one of my dad's students came up with."

"A money clip?" Andrew asked. "I think my dad has one of those. It just holds the dollar bills together so they don't get lost, right?"

"That's not all this one does," Kate said. "This one actually keeps track of how much money it's holding. It scans the bills. So let's say you reach for your wad of cash, wondering if you have enough to pay for a $25 item at the mall. This money clip will flash $27. Or $32. Or $40. Or whatever. You don't have to pull out the money and count it."

"That would save a lot of time, I guess," Andrew said. "And it wouldn't attract people's attention like standing there flashing money would."

"Yep, that's the idea behind most of these gadgets, actually," Kate said. "They just make life a little easier. And they're nifty."

"Nifty?" Sydney and Andrew spoke the word at the same time.

"Cool," Kate explained.

She pulled out a funny-looking pair of shoes. "These are different. One of my dad's students from last semester came up with these shoes with springs in the soles. They help people with joint pain in their knees and ankles. The springs relieve some of the tension as the person walks. Cool, huh?" She put on the shoes and began to walk with a spring in her step. . .literally. "They also make you run faster," she added.

"Ooh, I'd like to have a pair of those," Sydney said. "I run track, you know. Those shoes would make me lightning fast!"

"No doubt!" Kate pulled off the shoes and handed them to her friend. "Try them on. They're too big for me anyway."

Sydney slipped them on her feet. "Ooh, they're perfect! Just like in *Cinderella*."

"If the shoe fits. . . ," Andrew said with a grin.

"Keep them," Kate said with the wave of a hand. "My dad won't care. We have plenty more. And they will make you super-duper fast!"

"Wow!" Sydney stared at her feet. "Thank you so much.

I can't wait to run in them!" She looked around at all the gadgets then back at Kate. "I'm amazed by you! I never met anyone who knew so much about. . ." Sydney looked around. "About stuff."

Kate laughed. "Thanks, but it would really help me out a lot right now if I knew more about baseball, not electronics!"

Sydney stood and began to bounce up and down on her springy shoes. With a huge smile, she slung her arm over Kate's shoulder. "Aw, just leave the baseball stuff to me. I'll leave the technical stuff to you. We're gonna make a great team, short stuff!" Sydney said with a chuckle. "Just you wait and see!"

"Well, let's get going, then!" Kate said, feeling her excitement grow. "Let's solve this case!"

The Rumor Box

Kate grew more excited by the minute! The "Who Framed the Phillies Shortstop?" mystery had finally begun! Oh, she could hardly wait to get going!

"So where should we start?" Andrew asked, looking confused. "What do you two supersleuths think? Do you even think it's possible to track down the person who's framing my dad?"

Kate nodded. "Of course! And we'll start by going online and trying to find the source of the rumors. See who started all this stuff about your dad. Maybe getting that information will lead us to another clue, and then another, and then another! Before long, we'll have the case solved!"

"I wish I was as sure as you are." Andrew sighed.

"Well, keep praying," Kate encouraged him. "God already knows who did this, after all. If we pray for wisdom, He will give it to us. That's what the Bible says. So pray for wisdom! That's what we need to figure this out."

"Are you ready to start?" Sydney asked.

"You kids are welcome to use the Internet," Kate's mother said, entering the room. "Just don't stay on too long and only use the webcam if I'm close by. You can never be too careful, you know."

"Thanks, Mom." Kate went to the computer. "Andrew, where did you find that one article that upset you so much?" she asked. "I hate to ask you to look at it again, but it's important for us to find that Web site."

He gave her a blog address and she typed it in. When the Web page came up, she scrolled down until she saw the article about his father.

"Look right there," Andrew said. His brow wrinkled and Kate could tell he was upset.

They all leaned toward the monitor and Sydney read aloud: "Phillies fans got a wake-up call today when Tony Smith announced his unhappiness with playing for the team. According to Smith, 'I could have done better than these losers. And I plan to. . .next season when I move to a different town.' "

Sydney gasped. "That's horrible. And it really makes it sound like he said that."

"If I didn't *know* that it was a lie, I'd totally believe it," Kate said. "It sounds so real."

"But he *didn't* say it," Andrew insisted. "And it's not even true. My dad loves playing for the Phillies. Honest! And he loves living in Philadelphia. You should hear him talk about the historic district. And the Franklin Institute. And the Liberty Bell. He thinks this is the best place we've ever lived, and I agree!"

"We're going to get to the bottom of this, Andrew," Sydney promised. "So don't worry about what others are saying." She paused a moment then added, "Maybe that's a lesson God is trying to teach us. Maybe we're supposed to learn how to ignore it when others are talking about us, saying things we don't like. When the rumors get going, we just need to trust God. . .and not worry."

Kate scrolled down a bit more. "Look, here's another article," she said. "They took a picture of your dad looking mad and wrote a bunch of stuff about how he doesn't get along with his teammates. They make him sound like he's a real. . ." She paused then whispered, "Jerk."

"That's not true either." Andrew stood up and began to pace. "My dad is a great guy. And he's so nice to everyone. I don't know why anyone would say that."

"Oh, I know. I know." Kate nodded, hoping to reassure him.

"Man, but he looks really mad," Sydney observed. "I wonder why."

"I don't know." Andrew leaned down near the monitor and looked closely. "Hey, wait a minute! Look at that picture. Something about it doesn't seem right." He pointed. "The bottom part of the face doesn't even look like my dad's. Not at all. The chin is different." Andrew leaned in even closer. "This is *too* weird."

"Hang on a sec." Kate downloaded the photo and enlarged it until it filled the screen. "Ooh! Very sneaky. Check this out! This photo has been altered. It's only visible when the picture is enlarged like this, but you can see that the bottom half of the face is from one photo and the top from another." She stared at it in disbelief. How very strange that someone would take the time to do something like this. But why?

"Well, those are definitely my dad's eyes," Andrew said. "And his nose. So the top half is his face, but not the rest." Andrew made a fist and for a second Kate saw the anger in his eyes. "Why would someone do this to my dad? They would go so far as to forge a photograph? And misquote him? It's not right."

Sydney began to pace the room. "There's something more going on here than we know about. This isn't *just* about someone who doesn't like your dad. There's some reason why they want to see him gone from the team. Some bigger reason."

Andrew's eyes grew wide. "W—what are you thinking?"

"I'm not sure. Jealousy, maybe? Who knows? But someone with computer skills has gone out of his—or her—way to do this. We're dealing with someone very good at altering photographs."

"One of the other players, do you think?" Andrew suggested.

Kate shook her head. "That doesn't make any sense. Why would they do that? Besides, we'd better not assume it's one of the players. My dad says that's how the rumor mill gets started."

"Rumor mill?" Sydney and Andrew said at the same time.

"Gossiping," she explained. "Didn't you guys ever watch that VeggieTales episode when you were kids?"

"'Larry Boy and the Rumor Weed?'" Andrew's eyes widened. "Sure did! I have it memorized!" He burst into the theme song from the show and before long the girls were laughing.

"Well, it's kind of like that," Kate explained. "There's power in our words. Good and bad. So when we speak bad things over people—especially things that aren't true—it can really hurt. That's why it's so important not to gossip."

Sydney nodded. "And besides, there are enough rumors flying around already, so we have to be extra careful. We don't want to start any more. If we're not careful, we could end up blaming the wrong person. Imagine how bad that would be!"

"True, true." Andrew nodded.

"I have an idea!" Kate reached for a tissue from the box on the coffee table. "We need to start a rumor box."

"A rumor box?" Sydney gave her a curious look. "What's that?"

"Well, every time we hear a rumor, we'll stick it in the box and wait. If it's true, we'll pull it out of the box. And if it's not, we'll leave it in the box to remind us that it was just a rumor. That way we've protected someone who was innocent. So either way we win! And so does the person being talked about."

"Great idea," Sydney said. "Let's start by putting those rumors about Tony's teammates in there."

Kate ran into the garage and came back with a shoe box. "What about this? Do you think it will do?"

"Perfect!" Sydney said.

They wrapped the box in some old Mickey Mouse birthday paper and cut a hole in the top. Then Kate wrote on a piece of paper: "Rumor—Andrew's father doesn't like playing for the Phillies."

She folded up the paper and put it in the box. "There. We know *that* one's really a rumor, so it's in the box for good."

"Ooh! I have another one!" Sydney said. She grabbed a piece of paper and wrote, "Kate Oliver is the smartest girl in the world!" Then she grinned and said, "I made up that rumor myself. Hope it doesn't hurt your feelings, Kate."

"Hurt my feelings?" Kate laughed. "Not at all. And you can put it in the box, but I promise you, it's not true! There are a million zillion people smarter than me!"

"I haven't met any of them yet," Andrew said with a smile. His expression changed right away. "So now what do we do?" he asked, looking confused. "Just finding that blog site doesn't really tell us anything. How will we ever know who created it, or why they said all that stuff about my dad?"

"Hmm." Kate paused to think. "We have to figure out who owns these blogs and who's making these posts. And then we have to pay special attention at the games to look for anything—or anyone—suspicious."

"That's right," Andrew agreed. "There's really only one way to know for sure what's going on at a Phillies game. "We need to go to one. So are you girls on for Tuesday night?"

"Am I ever!" Sydney let out a whoop. "This is gonna be the greatest game in the history of mankind. We can do a little crime solving and game watching all at the same time. Talk about a winning combination."

Kate wasn't sure it sounded like so much fun. "I still can't figure out why everyone loves baseball so much." She groaned. "Just a bunch of guys running around a court to score points."

"Court?" Sydney snickered. "You mean *field*?"

"And they're not points, Kate," Andrew said. "They're runs."

"Court, field. Points, runs." She shrugged. "What's the difference?"

Sydney laughed as she looked at Andrew. "Man, oh man! Do we ever have our work cut out for us! Not only do we have to solve a mystery; we have to teach our friend here a little something about baseball."

"Hey now, don't you worry about me," Kate said, giving them a stern look. "If I can figure out how to use a computerized wristwatch, surely I can figure out a little something about a game like baseball. How hard can it be, after all?"

Sydney smiled. "Well, c'mon, then! What are we waiting for! Let's give this girl a crash course in baseball, Andrew."

Sydney began to search online for a baseball site. She finally found one titled EVERYTHING YOU EVER WANTED TO KNOW ABOUT BASEBALL BUT WERE AFRAID TO ASK. "Perfect!" she said, rubbing her hands together. "Now, let's get cracking! We've got a lot to learn, and only two days to learn it."

Kate groaned. In spite of Sydney and Andrew's excitement, she didn't really want to learn a lot about baseball. What was the point?

On the other hand, she did have a mystery to solve. Maybe. . .just maybe. . .she could learn a few things about baseball by Tuesday night. Then she and Sydney could crack this case wide open!

CHAPTER 5

Take Me Out to the Ballgame

On Tuesday evening, Kate arrived at Citizens Bank Park—the stadium where the Phillies played—with Sydney, Andrew, and Andrew's mom. The whole place seemed alive with excitement. Everywhere she looked, people rushed around with smiles on their faces.

Once inside, she looked up at the stadium, amazed at its enormous size! She'd never been inside such a huge place, especially one filled with so many people!

"Wow, this place is so large!" she said. "And it's so high tech!" Her eyes shifted this way and that, trying to take in everything at once, but it was too much.

"I can't believe you've never been here," Mrs. Smith said with a smile. "It's like a second home to us, now that my husband plays for the Phillies."

"I'm just not a big sports fan," Kate admitted. "But maybe it'll grow on me." She couldn't help but think that spending time in this stadium could make a fan out of just about anybody!

"Oh, I guarantee you'll fall in love with the Fightin' Phils in no time!" Mrs. Smith said, nodding. "We all have."

Kate thought about that a moment. Obviously the whole Smith family loved the Phillies. How could anyone say they didn't? Yes, all of this was surely just a big misunderstanding. And she would get to the bottom of it!

Sydney moved faster than everyone else, as always. Kate trudged along behind her, almost getting lost in the mob. She'd never seen so many people together in one place before. And most of them wore Phillies colors: red, white, and blue. She looked down at her orange shirt and pondered the fact that she looked different from everyone else in the crowd. Usually that didn't bother her. Kate never kept up with fashions, anyway. But tonight it suddenly seemed important to blend in.

Hmm. I'll have to do better next time.

Her glasses slipped down her nose and she pushed them back up with a sigh.

They worked their way through the hustle and bustle of the crowd, and then Mrs. Smith led them to their seats about ten rows behind the dugout. "What do you think of these, girls?"

"Oh, they're amazing, Mrs. Smith!" Sydney said. "I can't thank you enough. I can practically hear the players talking from here. And we're so close to the field! Oh, it makes me want to put on my new springy shoes and run out there!"

"Thanks again for inviting us." Kate looked around the stadium in awe. "This place is so cool. Look at all of those scoreboards. And the video screens! This is an electronic wonderland!" *Better than Disneyworld,* she decided.

Sydney just laughed. "You are so funny, Kate. This is a sports arena, not an electronics store! Enjoy the game!"

"Okay, I'll try." Kate shrugged and settled into her seat. She looked at the little area Mrs. Smith had called the dugout. Interesting. Small. Just big enough to fit the players inside. Kate wondered if they liked being in there. She started to ask Andrew but decided not to. He might make fun of her. Still, it might help solve the case to know what went on in the dugout. Maybe she could ask him about all of that later.

Mrs. Smith went to the concession stand to buy some sodas. Kate had never paid much attention to baseball before. Oh, sure. . .she'd seen a little when flipping channels on the television. And she had tried—really tried—to pay attention to the things that Sydney and Andrew had taught her the other night on the baseball Web site. But sitting here—listening to the roar of the crowd—was totally different. She could almost feel the energy in the air. And the voices of the crowd. . .wow! She'd never heard so many people talking together at the same time. It was hard to focus, for sure.

She looked around at all of the people. Several ate hot

dogs or popcorn. Yummy smells filled the air and made her tummy rumble. Mom had fixed an early dinner, but she could hardly stand to smell such great smells and not want more. In the distance, she saw a boy with nachos in his hand. *Yum!* She practically drooled just thinking about them. *Ooh! Look at that little girl over there.* She was nibbling on cotton candy. Where could Kate find some of that?

Just then, several children walked out onto the field. Even from Kate's seat close to the field, they looked pretty small. But why were they on the field? Surely they weren't baseball players. If so, then she really didn't know anything about this sport!

"Ooh, this should be good." Andrew jabbed her with an elbow. "The children's choir from a local school is singing the national anthem. I wonder if they're any good."

"Ah." So *that* explained it! Kate stood with the rest of the crowd and tried to imagine what it must feel like to be out there—looking at so many people. Were the children nervous? Would the players be nervous when the game began? Mr. Smith probably would be, since so many people were upset with him. Andrew said it had affected his game. That wasn't a good sign.

The voices of the children rose in beautiful harmony as they sang, "Oh, say, can you see, by the dawn's early light. . ."

As they continued, Kate pulled out her micro-sized digital camera. She zoomed in on them, looking at each child through the lens. In the middle of the first row, a little girl—shorter than all the others—sang with all of her heart. She had a face full of freckles. Kate liked her right away.

After the children sang, the audience members sat down. The ground below filled with men in uniforms. Several of them spread out and stood on little mats. They wore gloves on their right hands. Well, all but a couple, who wore them on their left hands. One guy stood in the middle of the grass with a ball in his hand and threw it at another guy with a bat. That guy hit it with a loud *smack* and the crowd roared. The ball flew through the air. . .way, way, way off in the distance.

The whole thing was captured on a giant screen that was raised above the outfield of the stadium. For a minute, Kate thought about the men working in the video room. . .wherever that was. What a cool job that would be!

"Wow, did you see that?" Sydney turned toward Kate with excitement in her eyes. "Jackson practically knocked it out of the park!"

"Oh, that's too bad," Kate said, frowning.

"No, that's *good*!" Andrew explained.

"So that's our guy?" Kate asked, pointing down to the field. "Right? The one in the white uniform running around the place mats?"

"Those are bases, Kate. Bases." Mrs. Smith gave her a funny look.

"Ah. Okay." She paused a moment then said, "Well, if he hit it out of the park, why are they making him run around all of those bases?"

Sydney turned to Kate, a stunned look on her face. "No. He has to get home!"

Andrew shook his head. "Just watch the game, Kate!"

She kept watching, but it just didn't make any sense. The little man in the white uniform circled the field below. Some of the men were jumping up and down, shouting. One was even throwing a ball at him. When he finished running, the crowd went wild, celebrating. Sydney, Andrew, and his mother all jumped up from their seats and started shouting.

"Did you see that?" Kate asked as they sat down again.

"What?" Sydney turned to look at her.

"That man. . .the one in the cool blue outfit with the number 14. He tried to hit our guy. He could have hurt him."

"Tried to throw him out, you mean," Sydney said with a nod.

"Out of the *game*?" Kate tried again.

"No." Sydney looked at Kate with a strange expression on her face. "Just *out*."

"Is that good?" Kate asked.

"Good?" Andrew stared at her like she had two heads. "Kate. . .Jackson just hit a homer!"

"A homer? *That's* good, right?" Kate shouted, hoping to be heard above the crowd.

It worked. The man in front of her turned around and stared.

"Oops." She smiled at him and shrugged.

"It's *very* good," Andrew whispered. "The Phillies are going to win this game if they keep playing like this. But can we talk about this later?"

"Sure." Kate sat quietly for a moment while the others watched the game. She reached into her bag and pulled out her tiny digital camera. Zooming in on the field, she snapped a couple of pictures of Andrew's dad as a ball whizzed across the field. He caught it and the crowd went crazy.

"Your husband is such a great player, Mrs. Smith," Sydney said.

"Thank you, honey. We think so."

After a few minutes, Kate couldn't resist talking. "So what's *he* doing?" she asked, pointing to the guy with the black shirt on the field below.

"That's the ump," Sydney responded. "He's officiating."

Kate gasped. Pushing up her glasses with her finger, she opened the camera once again and zoomed in on the ump for a closer look.

"What does that mean?" she asked.

"He's making the call," Sydney replied.

"Who's he calling?" Kate asked, snapping a photo.

"No, he's calling the shots," Andrew explained.

Sydney said, "Don't you remember anything we talked about the other night?"

"A little." Kate sighed. Loudly.

Kate looked around through her camera lens. When she tired of looking at faces in the crowd, she sat twiddling her thumbs, watching numbers light up the electronic board above.

"What does that mean?" she asked, pointing up at them.

Sydney groaned again. "Kate, I'm hungry. Would you please go and get me a hot dog and a drink?" She pulled some money out of her pocket and handed it over.

"Sure!" Kate answered, pleased to have something else to do, especially since it involved food. She looked up at the many, many people in the stadium. "Might take me awhile, though. Hope you don't mind."

"Oh, I don't mind. Take your time." Sydney turned back to the game.

"I'll come with you, Kate," Mrs. Smith said.

"Okay." As they left their seats, Kate noticed a man a few rows down standing with a camera in his hand, snapping pictures. Even from this distance, she could tell it was an expensive camera. *Wow. He must be a real fan.*

Something about the man caused a little shiver to run down her spine. What was it she had told Sydney and

Andrew again? *"The Bible says if you pray for wisdom, God will give it to you!"*

At once, she began to pray. If she ever needed wisdom, it was now!

A Face in the Crowd

Kate walked up, up, up the steps, through the maze of cheering fans, as she headed toward the concession stand. Mrs. Smith walked just behind her. All the way, Kate listened to the noise from the crowd. They finally located the snack area. The cashier was watching the game on the screen as Kate paid for Sydney's hot dog and soda. He yelped as the crowd in the stadium shouted in one loud voice.

"Struck him out!" the cashier hollered.

"Wow. I hope it didn't hurt!" Kate said, growing worried. Sounded pretty painful.

Mrs. Smith and the cashier each gave her a funny look. "No, honey," she explained. "He didn't actually *hit* him. Just. . .struck him out."

Kate just shrugged. With people saying so many confusing things, she was really starting to understand just how easily rumors could get started.

With food in hand, she followed Mrs. Smith back into the stadium. Kate managed to trip across nearly every toe in the row as she squeezed back down the crowded aisle toward Sydney and Andrew. They were both seated with their eyes glued to the field. Neither looked up as she sat down.

"Here you go," Kate said as she tried to hand Sydney the hot dog.

"Thanks, I'm not hungry," Sydney responded, eyes glued to the field.

"But I thought you said. . . Oh, never mind." Kate opened the hot dog wrapper and ate it herself. Just as she finished it, music began to play.

"Time for the seventh-inning stretch," Sydney said, standing.

"Seventh-inning stretch? Oh, okay." Kate stretched and let out a yawn. "There. That feels better. This game is making me sleepy anyway."

Andrew rolled his eyes and then laughed. "You're a hoot, Kate Oliver. You know that?"

The game started again. As it continued, Kate tried to pay attention. She really tried. But the whole thing was just so. . .boring. Why did baseball move so slowly? These guys seemed to take forever to get from one place mat to the next. Why didn't they just go all the way at once?

Oh well. There were more exciting things to do, right? She used the zooming feature on her micro-camera to watch the people in the crowd. She wasn't sure what she was looking for. Her gaze stopped on that suspicious-looking man with the camera about three rows below. He wasn't taking pictures anymore. No, this time he had something very small in his hand.

"What is that?" She zoomed in a little better to see. Looked like an MP3 player of some sort. Why would someone bring a music player to a game? Seemed a little odd. Unless he was bored like her, of course. But he looked like someone who cared a lot about the game.

Hmm. Kate sure couldn't tell much from behind him, but something about the man made her uncomfortable.

Just then, the crowd shrieked and the man dropped whatever he was holding. He slipped out of his seat and reached to grab it. A look of relief passed over his face as soon as he held it in his hand again.

"Whatever it is must be pretty important," Kate whispered. She made a mental note to bring her Internet wristwatch next time she came to the game. It would sure come in handy for looking things up—like that MP3 player, for instance. "I wonder what brand it is," she whispered.

"Did you say something?" Sydney looked at her curiously.

"Oh, nothing important." She shrugged and tried to tuck away her curiosity to pay attention to her friend.

"Look," Sydney said, jumping with glee. "It's Tony Smith's turn at bat." She clapped her hands together with a nervous look on her face. "Oh, I hope he hits a homer!"

Kate zoomed in to get a good look, even taking a couple of pictures for good measure. When Tony's first swing missed the ball, the crowd reacted with a loud boo. "Why are they so mean?" Kate asked. It hardly seemed fair. The whole crowd seemed to be against him. Why would they turn on one of their own players like that?

"Maybe he'll hit the next one," Sydney said. "He's a shortstop, but he's also a great hitter. Usually." She began to bite her nails, looking more nervous by the second.

"Shortstop?" Kate looked at her curiously. "I heard you say that before. But what does it mean? What's a shortstop?"

Sydney answered but never took her eyes off of Tony. "A shortstop is the guy who stands between second and third base. Out there," she said, pointing to the field. "That's a really important defensive position in baseball. More balls go to the shortstop than anyone else."

"Wow. So he must be good."

"Yep! He's great!" Sydney said.

Unfortunately, Tony took a swing at the next ball and missed it, too.

Sydney groaned, but the crowd's reaction was even worse. This time they got really upset. A fan behind them yelled something mean about Mr. Smith, and Kate turned to give him a "Shame on you" look. He didn't even notice.

"I'm telling you. . .Tony is the best," Sydney insisted. "That's what's so confusing about all of this."

"I think he's just nervous because of the way people are shouting at him," Andrew explained. "My dad hardly ever misses."

Thankfully, the third time the ball came right for the center of Mr. Smith's bat. Kate found herself chanting, "Hit it! Hit it!" along with Sydney.

"You can do it, Dad," Andrew said. "C'mon!"

As if he heard his son, Tony Smith cracked the bat against the ball and it shot off into space. Well, not space, exactly, but way across the court. Or was it *field*?

"He did it! He did it! He did it!" Sydney yelled. She let out a loud yelp and Kate put her fingers in her ears.

As the crowd began to cheer, Tony ran to first base, then second, where he stopped for a split second. His gaze darted to the right, then to the left. Finally he took off running again, making it to third, just in the nick of time before the guy on the base caught the ball in his glove.

"Safe!" a loud voice shouted.

"Wow! That's so cool!" For the first time, Kate felt excited about the game! Maybe sports weren't all bad, after all. Maybe she just hadn't given them a real chance before.

Andrew looked at her with a smile on his face. "Now we're talking!"

"Great hit," Sydney agreed with a huge smile on her face.

The next batter hit the ball the wrong way, and it came flying into the stands near Kate and the others. She squealed as it flew over her head. The announcer hollered, "Foul!"

"Man!" Kate started shaking. "I didn't know baseball was such a dangerous game! And what's all this stuff about a foul ball? What does that mean?"

"It means the ball went the wrong way," Sydney explained.

The camera zoomed in on a man above them, who caught the foul ball. He had a big smile on his face. Kate wasn't so sure what he was happy about. She wouldn't be smiling if someone hit her with a ball that went the wrong way, especially one flying so fast! Still, everyone else seemed to think it was wonderful.

The cheering died down and the game started up once again. Minutes later, the crowd began to cheer. Their shouts filled the stadium from top to bottom, side to side. Kate could hardly hear herself think, the noise was so loud!

"We're going to win this one!" Andrew shouted above the roar of the people around them. "Put another one in the win column for the Fightin' Phils!"

Sure enough, the Phillies won the game. The people all around Kate began to celebrate wildly. She'd never heard such excitement. Crazy, how people could get so worked up over a game.

Well, all but one person. She glanced down at the man

she'd been watching all evening. He sure didn't look happy the Phillies had won. . .but why? Wasn't he a fan?

Hmm. Very interesting.

After a minute or two of thinking about that, Kate joined in the frenzy, shouting and cheering. "If you can't beat 'em, join 'em!" she said, then giggled.

"Let's go down to the dugout and say hi to my dad," Andrew said. He led the way through the crowd down the stairs. Kate followed him. She stopped cold when the saw the man in the red shirt up close. He tucked something into his pocket then turned her way with a cold stare.

"What's your problem, kid?" he asked.

"I, um. . .nothing." She tried to dart past him, but the camera in her hand fell to the cement. She grabbed the phone and ran to the dugout, ready to be away from the creepy fellow! Something about him gave her cold chills all over. *Brr!*

When they reached the dugout, she watched the other players congratulating each other. However, she noticed no one said much to Tony Smith. Kate had to wonder about that. *Why are they ignoring him? He played well, too.*

Were they really *that* upset with him? She watched awhile longer, noticing people from the stands asking for autographs. They went up to all of the players except Tony. The sad expression on his face almost made Kate cry.

Why are they treating him this way? Can't they see that

he loves this team. . .that he's giving 100 percent? Don't they care that he played well? That he's working overtime to be the best he can be?

Suddenly she felt very, very sorry for Mr. Smith. Just then he looked her way and smiled. "Hey, Kate. Thanks for coming."

"You're welcome, Mr. Smith," she said, feeling her spirits lift. "It was a great game. You were terrific." She gave him her biggest possible smile.

"Thanks." He looked embarrassed. "But please call me Tony. That's all I am. Just Tony."

"Tony the Tiger!" Andrew said with a smile. "That's what most of his fans call him."

Mr. Smith shrugged. "Well, some of the fans, anyway. Not everyone."

"Tony the Tiger! I *love* it!" Sydney shoved her way ahead of Kate, her black braids bobbing up and down as she headed straight to Mr. Smith. "You're the best shortstop ever, Mr. Smith. Can I please have your autograph? I'll treasure it forever and ever!"

"Well, of course." He took the program from Sydney and signed it with a smile. "I'm honored." After handing it back to her, he looked at all of them with a twinkle in his eye. "Now, who wants some ice cream? My treat."

"Really, Dad?" Andrew asked. "You have time for that?"

"Sure." His dad nodded. "I've been too distracted with

practice lately. Need a nice outing with family and friends."

Sydney's eyes grew wide. "Wow!" She looked like she might faint. "I'm really going out to have ice cream with a sports star. Can you believe it? This is one of the coolest things that's ever happened to me!"

"I'm no star." Mr. Smith gave them a sheepish look.

"Well, sure you are! And I can't wait to tell my friends back home about this." Sydney chattered on about how cool it was, but Kate was distracted, staring at her camera. Somehow, when it had fallen to the floor, it had taken a picture of the man. She could barely make out his face because of the strange angle, but something about it just scared her. A chill ran up her spine and goose bumps covered her arms. She wondered why looking at him made her feel so nervous.

She shook off her fear as she whispered a prayer. No point in worrying about someone she didn't even know, right? Besides, there would be plenty of time to think about that later. Right now, she had some ice cream to eat!

A Brilliant Beyond Brilliant Idea

The morning after the ballgame, Kate woke up bright and early with a great idea. She rolled over in the bed and stared at Sydney, who slept like a rock. "C'mon, wake up," she whispered. "I need to talk to you. Wake up, wake up, wake up!"

Sydney opened sleepy eyes. "I'm awake now." She groaned. "What time is it, anyway?"

"Seven thirty," Kate said, glancing at the clock. "I know it's early, but this is really important!"

"Ugh." Sydney put the pillow over her face and groaned again. "What is it about you and mornings? Don't you ever sleep in? It's summer, remember?"

"Don't you like to get up in the mornings and run?" Kate asked.

"Yes, but not this early!"

"It's just. . .we have too much work to do, and I've had a brilliant beyond brilliant idea." Kate giggled with excitement. "I think you're gonna love it!"

That seemed to get Sydney's attention. She pulled the pillow back and stared at Kate with a curious look on her face. "Oh?"

"We need to start a new blog site," Kate explained.

"A blog? You mean, like a Web page?"

"Sort of. Blogs are a little different from Web sites. A blog is really more like an online journal. Kind of like a diary, almost. It's the same basic idea as a Web page, but we would update it every day and write cool articles and stories and stuff." Kate bounced up and down, thinking about the possibilities. It all made perfect sense.

"So why do we need this blog site, again?" Sydney asked with a yawn. She swung her legs over the side of the bed and stood up.

"Well, think about it. If we start a Phillies blog and write great stories and articles about Tony Smith, maybe the person who's trying to frame him will *see* our site and leave comments."

"Probably not *good* comments," Sydney said, shivering. "It might get kind of ugly." She began to do stretches, leaning to the right, then the left, then right and left again.

"Doesn't matter." Kate pushed back the covers and scrambled out of the bed to stand next to her. For fun, she did a couple of stretches, too. "We don't have to worry about what he or she says. We just want that person to post so we can track him—or her—down through the Web.

There are ways to do that. I think I can figure it out if I take my time."

"So how do we do it? Build the blog, I mean." Sydney looked like she wasn't sure about all this. She spread out her arms and began to do jumping jacks.

Kate decided to join her. "B–building the b–blog won't be the p–problem!" Kate huffed and puffed as she jumped up and down. "I've b–built Web sites before." She stopped jumping and bent over, panting. After a minute, she rose up and stared at Sydney, who continued doing jumping jacks. "I did our school's Web site."

"Of course!" Sydney dropped down to the ground and began to do sit-ups. "I'm sure it'll be great, if you're making it!"

"Should be easy." Kate pushed up her glasses. "But this Phillies site will be a little different because I don't know much about the team. I guess it would help to know a little something about them. How much can you tell me, Sydney?"

"Quite a bit," her friend said, bobbing up and down on the floor. "But since I'm not from Philly, it might help to have Andrew help us."

"Or. . .the Camp Club Girls!" Kate rose from the bed and began to pace the room. "While we're concentrating on the problem, they can help us."

"What? We'll ask them to go ahead and do the research we need?" Sydney said. She rolled over onto her stomach and started doing push-ups. "Wait, I thought I wasn't the only one who was out of town this week. . . ."

"Yes," Kate said. "I think nearly all of them are out of town. I think Elizabeth is home but helping out at her church's VBS, so I don't think she's available much either. So we may not have our normal contact with the rest of the girls, but we can try to talk to them at night, I guess."

"Sounds like a plan." Now Sydney was huffing and puffing. Still, she never lost count as she pushed up, down, up, down.

"Probably someone will be able to help us learn more about the Phillies. Then we'll have some good stuff to put in our blog. The girls will find all the statistics and quotes we need to put together great stories and articles. In the meantime, let's go downstairs and eat breakfast; then we'll get busy on that blog site."

"Okay, just twenty more!"

Sydney finished her exercise routine; then they raced down the stairs, almost tripping over Dexter, who played with his electronic car on the bottom step. "Hey, watch where you're going!" he cried out. "You could've stepped on my car."

"Sorry, Dex," Kate said. "We have work to do. But first things first!"

They went into the kitchen and fixed bowls of cereal. Kate filled her bowl to the top, but Sydney carefully measured out a small portion.

"This stuff has a lot of sugar in it," she said. "So I'll just cut back a little on how much I eat."

"Okay. Whatever." Kate shoveled in big spoonfuls of the crunchy stuff, talking with her mouth full. "This will be great, Sydney. I love being a detective, don't you? Like Nancy Drew, even!" She took another bite then added, "Oh, and guess what? Maybe after we figure out who's doing this to Tony Smith, we'll be on the news. We could be famous."

"Supersleuths forever!" Sydney shouted.

"Supersleuths forever!" Kate echoed with a giggle.

Sydney sipped her orange juice and her eyebrows shot up. "Hey! Maybe the newspaper will want to write an article on my sports connection. I've played softball, you know. And I'm going to be in the Olympics someday." She began to talk about all of the things she hoped to do before she turned twenty, but Kate had a hard time keeping up. Her thoughts were on the blog they were going to start after breakfast.

"True, true." Kate took another big bite of the sweet cereal and then paused to think about that. "This is so exciting! Supersleuths of America, unite!"

"Go, Inspector Gadget!" Sydney hollered. "We're going to be famous!"

Kate laughed and finished eating. As she rinsed out her cereal bowl, her mother entered the kitchen.

"You girls are up early. I'd planned to make French toast. Looks like I'm too late."

"French toast?" Kate's mouth began to water. "Yum! I'm not full. What about you, Sydney?"

"Well. . ." Sydney didn't look so sure.

"Aw, come on! My mom makes the best French toast in Pennsylvania," Kate said. "Don't you have room for at least one piece? Or two? I could eat a dozen!"

"I don't know how you do it," Kate's mother said. "You must have a hollow leg."

"A hollow leg?" Kate stared down at her legs. "What do you mean?"

Her mother laughed. "That's just something my mom used to say. It means I can't figure out where you're putting all of that food you eat! Your stomach surely isn't big enough, so you must have a hollow leg it goes into."

"Oh, I don't know." Kate shrugged. "I'm just always hungry. But maybe I'm about to go through a growing spell or something." She laughed. "Maybe by next week I'll be six feet tall!"

"Now, *that* would be a story for the papers!" Sydney said, snickering.

Kate looked at her friend and sighed. Sydney was so great at eating only healthy foods. And she was so tall and muscular. So athletic. Maybe that was the way to grow taller—to eat only healthy foods and to exercise a lot. Oh well. Not everyone had to have muscles, right?

Dexter joined them at the table. He put his battery-operated car on top of the wooden table and pressed a button on the remote control. It raced across the table and over the edge, into Kate's lap.

"Better watch out, Dex," she cautioned. "If you keep running over me with this car of yours, I'm going to confiscate it."

"Confiscate?" He looked at her curiously. "What's confiscate?"

"It means she's going to take it and keep it," Sydney explained. "You'll never see it again."

Dexter's eyes widened. "No way!" He snatched the car and put it on the counter nearby, then watched it as he ate.

They enjoyed some warm, yummy French toast. Kate ate until she was very full.

Biscuit came to the side of the table and whined. Kate tore off a tiny piece of the French toast and slipped it to him, hoping no one would notice. He gobbled it up and cried for more.

"Shh," Kate whispered. "You'll get me in trouble!"

"I heard that," her mom said. "Don't you feed that dog any more table scraps, Kate Oliver. He's going to end up chubby."

"Chubby? Biscuit?" She looked at him and shrugged. Maybe he had put on a couple of pounds since coming to live with her, but surely a few nibbles of people food couldn't hurt him.

After eating, Kate decided it was time to work on their new Phillies blog site. She signed onto the Web then went to her favorite blogging site and clicked the START A NEW BLOG button. Over the next half hour, she and Sydney put together a cool-looking site filled with the Phillies colors— red, white, and blue. With her friend's help, Kate added some basic information about the ball team.

"I'll fill in the side panels with information later," Kate explained, "but this is enough for now." She paused a moment then added, "But now we need to write something really cool about Tony Smith. . .something to convince fans he's a great guy!"

"Well, you heard all that stuff he said the other night when we were eating ice cream—how he loves playing baseball." Sydney nodded. "How he's played since he was a kid? I'm sure he wouldn't mind if we used some of the things he said."

"Great idea!" Kate quickly wrote the title to a new article: TONY SMITH—A PLAYER PHILLIES FANS CAN TRUST.

"This article should do it," Katie said. "I'll bet that person who's been writing the bad things about Tony is watching the Web to see what others say. So this article we write will be like putting out bait. I'll bet he writes some sort of comment." She paused a moment. "But we need a lot more information about Tony. Good stuff."

"We need actual quotes," Sydney said with a sparkle in her eye. "More specific stuff than what he shared after the game. Stuff about the team, and about how much he loves his teammates and his coaches. And Philadelphia! We really need to play up the Philadelphia connection. This is the City of Brotherly Love, you know."

"Yes, I know." Kate grinned. "I've lived here all my life, remember?"

"Oh yeah." Sydney gave her a sheepish look. "So do you think Tony will give us an interview? We could be, like. . .reporters!" Sydney smiled. "I always thought it'd be fun to be a sports reporter, and now I get to be, thanks to this Web site!"

"*Blog* site," Kate corrected her. "And I don't know if he'll give us an interview or not. Maybe we could call Andrew and ask."

Just then the phone rang. Kate looked down at the caller ID, noticing Andrew's number. She stared back up at her friend, stunned.

"Wow!" Kate and Sydney looked at each other.

"It's like a miracle," Kate whispered. "God was listening to us."

"He's *always* listening to us!" Sydney echoed. "But that's extra super cool."

Kate picked up the phone and started talking fast. "Hey,

Andrew. I'm so glad you called. We were just talking about you. Sydney and I are starting a blog site and we need your help. Do you think your dad will give us an interview? We really need to get some great quotes to put in our first article."

"Probably, but there's something happening right now, Kate. Turn on the radio."

"The radio?" she asked. "What station?"

He told her, and Kate turned it on right away. She heard a man's voice saying, "Ladies and gentlemen, I guess this confirms the rumors we've been hearing about Tony Smith's thoughts on playing for the Phillies. You heard it in his own words."

"Heard *what* in his own words?" Kate said. She turned her attention back to the phone. "What was it, Andrew? Your dad was on the radio?"

"No." Andrew sounded more upset by the minute. "That's just it. He *wasn't* on the radio. He never gave an interview, I mean. But it *was* his voice. How did they do that?"

"Wait. You're saying they found someone with a voice like his who pretended to be him?"

"No, that's the crazy part. It really was my dad's voice. We all heard it, and even my mom said so. We know his voice. My dad is so upset right now."

"Of course, but. . ." Kate exhaled loudly. "It just doesn't

make any sense. First people start rumors about him, and now his voice is on the radio, telling people the rumors are true?"

"Yes. But it doesn't make any sense."

"No kidding." She sat on the edge of the bed. "Andrew, we're going to get to the bottom of this, I promise. Someone taped your dad's voice without his knowing it."

"But how? And when? He hasn't given any interviews in weeks, not since all the rumors started. Coach Mullins told him not to. Said the reporters would twist his words. So he's stayed away from reporters. He's already really upset. You know he's been working with that charity for kids with muscular dystrophy, right?"

"Of course!" Kate knew all about it. The top secret project she and her father had been working on was a special robot to help kids with muscular problems. She hadn't told a soul yet, not even Sydney or the other Camp Club Girls. First they had to work out some of the kinks. There was no point in getting people excited about something that might not even work.

"My dad's worried that the people at the Muscular Dystrophy Foundation won't trust him now," Andrew said, sounding sad.

"Why would he think that?" Kate asked.

"Because it's already happening. Have you seen that bank commercial my dad is in?"

"Sure, I see it all the time. I love the part where your dad says, 'A penny saved is a penny earned.' That's a Ben Franklin quote, you know."

"Yeah, I know. But you won't hear my dad saying that anymore. The president of the bank just called and said they're not running the commercial anymore. They're taking it off the air because they think my dad is bad for business."

"Oh, Andrew! I'm so sorry. But I'll be praying, I promise. And we're going to do everything we can to fix this. With God's help, I mean." Kate paused a minute. "When is the next game?"

"Saturday afternoon."

"Can you get tickets?"

"We have season tickets. Four seats. So that's not a problem."

"Good ones?" she asked. "Close to the dugout?"

"Well, sure. Same seats as last time. We always sit in the same place. But what are you thinking?"

"I'm thinking I'd better learn a lot more about the team before I go. In the meantime, just stay calm. Oh, and write down everything you know about the Phillies for our blog, okay? And it would be great if you could get a couple of quotes from your dad, telling how much he loves the team. We'll use those in our articles."

"O–okay." He sighed.

"I'm so sorry about all of this, Andrew. But don't worry. God has this under control. I know we can trust Him."

"I know. It's just hard."

"Well, let's pray about it, then." Kate began to pray out loud over the phone, something she'd never done before. It made her feel really good to pray for Andrew, and by the time they hung up, she could tell he felt a little better.

Afterward, Kate put the phone down on the desk and looked at Sydney with a dramatic sigh.

"What happened?" Sydney asked, her brow wrinkling in concern. "Sounds bad."

"Yes, it is. What a mess! Someone is really working hard to make Mr. Smith look bad. And it's working. The bank just canceled a commercial he's in. And Andrew's afraid it's going to get even worse—that the people at the Muscular Dystrophy Foundation will drop him as a spokesman, too."

"This is just so sad."

"Yes," Kate agreed. "We need to find out how someone taped Tony's voice without his knowing. That's the only way we'll ever get to the bottom of this."

Sydney began to pace the room. "Man! Do you think it was a reporter? Maybe someone snuck in the locker room or something? Or. . ." Her face lit up. "Maybe someone tapped his phone. What do you think?"

"I don't know, but I'm going to get to the bottom of this," Kate said. "Let's send an e-mail to the other Camp

Club Girls. We need their help. This is too much for the two of us to handle on our own."

"Good idea," Sydney said.

Kate sat down at the computer. She began to write an e-mail to the Camp Club Girls.

Dear Bailey, Alex, Elizabeth, and McKenzie:
Please meet me in the Camp Club Girls chat room tonight at 7:00 eastern time. A mystery awaits! Sydney and I need you. . .ASAP!

As she clicked the SEND button, Kate leaned back in her chair and smiled. "There! That should do it! If anyone can get to the bottom of this mystery, the Camp Club Girls can!"

Camp Club Girls. . .Unite!

Kate and Sydney spent the rest of the day at the pool, swimming with Dexter. It was nice to enjoy some fun time. Kate thought about the first time she met Sydney and the other Camp Club Girls at Discovery Lake Camp. What fun they'd had, solving their first case and getting to know each other. Now they were all great friends. And on days like today, swimming with Sydney, Kate could almost forget the Phillies and all of the problems Andrew and his dad were going through.

Almost.

After a few minutes of fun, Sydney announced, "I need to swim one hundred laps. Hope you don't mind, but I want to make the swim team this year and I need to work on my speed and strength."

Kate shrugged. "Okay. No problem." She went to the shallow end and sat on the steps. Two women her mother's age sat on the steps next to her. She couldn't help but hear their conversation.

"They need to kick that Tony Smith off the team," a woman in a black bathing suit said. She fanned herself with her hand and rolled her eyes. "Seriously, he needs to find someplace else to go!"

The other woman—dressed in a green suit—reached for a diet soda and took a sip. She shook her head and said, "He's hurting the morale of the other players. His attitude is terrible! And lately he hasn't even played well!"

"Excuse me. . . ," Kate started to say.

The woman looked her way. "Yes?" the lady in the black suit said. "Can we help you?"

"Oh. . .never mind."

Kate wanted to explain that it was all a big mistake—that Tony actually loved the Phillies—but decided not to. It would be better to prove them wrong than to tell them they were wrong. And she would do that—with the help of her friends.

The afternoon ended too quickly. Kate's mom and dad took the girls out to eat at an all-you-can-eat pizza buffet that evening.

"I love, love, love this place!" Kate said as they entered. She stopped inside the door and drew in a deep breath. "Do you smell that? Do you? It's the most wonderful smell in the world. Smell the garlic? Smell the pizza crust baking? Smell the pepperoni and sausage? Oh, I think that's the best smell ever!"

"You're funny! You know that?" Sydney laughed. "Just smells like pizza to me. But look at that salad bar! They have great veggies. I'm going to love this place."

"Veggies?" This was one of Kate's favorite places to eat, but she'd never noticed the vegetables before. Oh well. She grabbed a plate and got in line. She loaded up on the good stuff. . .three pieces of sausage pizza, one slice of pepperoni, a bowl of spaghetti and meatballs, and two slices of dessert pizza.

Sydney grabbed a bowl and filled it with salad, loading it with bright orange carrot sticks, round red tomatoes, and lots of green cucumbers. Afterward, she took a tiny slice of cheese pizza.

Kate looked at her, stunned. "That's all you're eating?"

"Sure." Sydney shrugged. "Why?"

"Oh, no reason." Kate tried not to feel bad about all of the food she ate as they shared the meal together, but she had to wonder if she was the only one who loved pizza. She even made a second trip back to the buffet for two more slices of pepperoni. Her mother looked at her and said, "Hollow leg!" Kate just laughed.

They arrived home at ten minutes until seven.

"Don't forget to feed Biscuit," Kate's mom said. "And take him outside for a few minutes."

Kate filled Biscuit's bowl with food and watched as he chomped it down. "Slow down, boy! You'll end up weighing a ton! You won't be a very good crime solver if you're too chubby to chase the bad guys!"

Biscuit never even looked up from his food. He just kept eating and eating.

Afterward, Kate took him outside. Sydney went with her. They stood in the backyard talking about the case while Biscuit roamed the yard and chased a squirrel. From inside the house, Kate heard the grandfather clock chime seven times.

"Oh! We're supposed to be online to meet the other girls!"

They raced back inside, where Kate signed onto the Internet. She giggled as she entered the chat room. Bailey—the youngest in their group—was already there.

> Bailey: *Hey Freckles! Whazup? U said it was important!*
> Kate: *Wait till the others sign on. I'll tell u everything, I promise. Something is happening and we need ur help!*
> Bailey: *Okie dokie.*

"Who is it?" Sydney asked, settling into the chair next to Kate.

"Bailey." Kate pointed at the screen. "She's the first one to sign on."

"Of course!" Sydney laughed. "Bailey might be the

youngest, but she's always ready to roll!"

A few seconds later, Alex signed into the chat room. Kate smiled when she saw her name. Alex knew everything there was to know about solving tough cases. Surely she would be able to help!

Next Elizabeth Anderson signed on. Elizabeth was fourteen—older than any of the others. She always knew just what to do. Kate had enjoyed getting to know Elizabeth at camp. She was so mature, and loaded with godly wisdom!

At five minutes after seven, McKenzie joined them. McKenzie was thirteen and never gave up on a case, even a really tough one like this. Kate could hardly wait to share the news.

McKenzie: *What's up?*

Kate quickly filled them in on the story, sharing everything about Tony Smith and his problems with the team. Afterward, she typed, *We need all of you!*

Elizabeth: *We're here! Whatever u need, just tell us!*
Kate: *Sydney and I have assignments for you.*
     How do u feel about that?
McKenzie: *Gr8!*
Bailey: *Cool! Assign away, oh Chief.*

Kate smiled as she typed.

> Kate: *McKenzie, you're a deep thinker. And you're so smart! We need you to think of all the reasons why someone would want to do this to Mr. Smith.*
>
> McKenzie: *I'll put on my thinking cap.*
>
> Kate: *Alex, you're so encouraging! We want you to put together a team of kids to write letters of encouragement to Mr. Smith. Those letters will lift his spirits, and he really needs that right now.*
>
> Alexis: *Sounds like fun.*
>
> Kate: *Elizabeth, you're such a prayer warrior. I would feel better if I knew lots of people were praying! Could you help with that? Put together a prayer team, maybe?*
>
> Elizabeth: *I'd be happy to! I'll ask lots of people to pray at certain times of day.*
>
> Bailey: *What about me? What can I do?*
>
> Kate: *Keep posting comments to our new Phillies blog. Write some great things about Tony Smith. Let people know what a terrific guy he is. It would be great if all of you could do that. . .and ask your friends and family members to post their comments, too. The more, the better! Just ask them to say nice things only. Okay?*

Kate quickly gave them the link to the new site and they all agreed to help.

> Kate: *We also need someone to do some research on the Phillies and their history. We also need good stuff on Tony Smith, like how much he's helped kids with muscular dystrophy. . .that sort of thing. Internet searches may be enough, but it may also mean a trip to the library. Anyone game?*
>
> Bailey: *I can do that, too. I'll dig out Phillies info, Philly Queen Mystery Solver! My fam is going to Chicago this weekend, so I'll look at one of the big libraries there.*
>
> Alexis: *And I can help by finding out stuff about Tony Smith.*

As they ended the chat, Kate turned to Sydney.

"What do you think?" she asked. "What else can we do? It will be a few days before Bailey gives us information. And it'll take awhile for the rest of the Camp Club Girls to get going, too. What can we do. . .right here, right now?"

"Hmm." Sydney wrinkled her nose as she thought about it. "I suppose we should find some local people who Tony Smith has helped in some way. Get some personal interviews of lives he's touched."

"Great idea!" Kate agreed. "And when we're done with that, let's figure out the best possible way to get people to notice our new blog site."

"How do we do that?" Sydney asked.

"It's not as hard as you think. Just takes time." With the wave of a hand, Kate explained, "I can announce the site to all of my friends here in Philadelphia and ask them to send the link to their friends, and their friends' friends, and so on. Before long, people all over the country will know! Also, I'll go to some of the other Phillies blog sites—the ones saying the bad stuff about Mr. Smith—and leave comments with a link to our site. That'll get 'em there, I'm sure!"

"I'll do the same thing," Sydney agreed. "I know lots of people who love sports. As soon as our blog site is up and going full speed, I'll send the link. Before long, we'll have the best Phillies site on the World Wide Web!"

Kate couldn't help but laugh. "It's funny, isn't it? A few days ago I knew nothing about baseball. And now I'm writing about it. Go figure!"

"It's all for a worthy cause," Sydney said with a nod. "And besides, you'll fall in love with baseball, I promise. It's such a great sport. And with players like Tony Smith, what's not to love?"

Kate shrugged. She still wasn't so sure about the whole baseball thing. But maybe next Saturday's game would be the true test. Perhaps there she could solve a mystery—and at the same time fall in love with the game of baseball!

Supersleuths on the Job!

On Saturday afternoon, Kate and Sydney went back to the stadium for another Phillies game with Mrs. Smith and Andrew. Kate deliberately wore a red, white, and blue T-shirt and a pair of jeans. She wanted to fit in with the other fans this time—not stick out like a sore thumb in a bright orange shirt! Besides, this whole sports thing was beginning to rub off on her. Sort of, anyway. She was actually starting to get excited about baseball! And solving the case, of course. She could hardly wait to do that! Whoever was framing Tony Smith would soon be caught if she had anything to do with it.

They entered the stadium to the strains of "Take Me Out to the Ballgame." Hearing the song made happiness rise in Kate's heart. How exciting!

Sydney's face was practically shining with joy. "I love, love, love coming here!" she said with a squeal. "But you're going to have to keep an eye on me, Kate, 'cause I'm gonna get caught up in the game and forget we're supposed to be crime solving! You know how I am! I might be a supersleuth, but I'm also a sports fan!"

"Of course! But I won't let that happen. Inspector Gadget is on the job!" Kate giggled. "I've got my dad's super-high-strength binoculars, and I brought my tiny digital camera again, just in case I see anything strange. Plus—and this is really cool—I've got my Internet watch. I'm ready no matter what comes our way!"

"I still can't believe you can read Web pages on a wristwatch," Andrew said, shaking his head.

"What are we looking for exactly, though?" Sydney asked.

"Well, maybe a nosy reporter hanging out around the locker room," Kate explained. "Or one of the players in the dugout acting suspicious. Anything, really."

"Before the game starts, let's pray, okay?" Sydney said. " 'Cause I know we need God's help with this. It's too big for us to solve by ourselves."

"Sure!" Kate agreed.

Once they settled into their seats, Kate bowed her head and Sydney said a quick prayer. Even though it was super loud in the stadium, Kate felt sure God still heard them loud and clear!

After praying, Andrew headed to the dugout to say hello to his father. Kate watched him wind his way through the many, many fans to get to the small dugout area.

What would it feel like, to have a sports hero for a father? Especially now with people saying so many mean things about him?

Kate could sort of imagine what it felt like to have a famous father. Her dad was going to be famous when SWAT-bot hit the stores! Not that he needed to be famous to impress her. She already thought he was the very best dad in the world.

Minutes later, Andrew returned to his seat looking sad. "I told my dad to have fun," he said, taking his seat. "He said it's getting harder with each game, but I just reminded him that he loves the sport. And I told him about that Bible verse we learned at church last week."

"Which one? I don't remember." Kate gave him a curious look.

"You know—that one that says blessed are you when men persecute you and say bad things against you?"

"Oh yeah!" Kate remembered. "Well, that one certainly applies, doesn't it!"

"Well, my dad is being falsely accused. And with all of these rumors flying around, he's really being persecuted by others. So he *must* be mighty blessed."

"That's a great way to look at it," Kate agreed.

"He should just relax and have a great game," Sydney said, wrinkling her nose. "He can't control what other people are thinking, anyway."

"Yeah, but I still wish they wouldn't think bad things about him or *say* bad things about him. I know it hurts his feelings. . .and mine, too!" Andrew sighed. Kate felt bad for him.

"I guess God is teaching us all a lesson about spreading rumors, isn't He?" she said. "Maybe that's the point of all of this—to show us just how wrong it is to talk about people behind their backs, especially when it's not true!"

"I'll be a lot more careful about who I talk about, that's for sure," Sydney said. "I'll think before I speak even if I don't know the person."

"Me, too," Andrew agreed.

"No more talking about people behind their backs!" Kate announced in her strongest voice.

"Speaking of not talking about people behind their backs. . ." The woman in front of them had turned around with a stern look. "Would you kids mind being a little quieter during this game? Last time one of you was shouting in my ear through the whole game." She looked at Sydney, who put her hand over her mouth.

"Oops! Sorry," Sydney said. "But I'm such a big fan! I can hardly control myself. Especially when Tony Smith is on the field."

At the mention of Tony's name, the woman rolled her eyes and mumbled some not-so-nice things. She turned back around to face the field.

"Never mind all that," Kate whispered to Andrew. "She'll be a fan of your dad's again, too, after we solve this case."

Several rows down, something caught Kate's eye. She watched as a man in his late twenties stood and pulled something out of his pocket. *Hmm.* Something about him seemed strange. He turned her way for a moment and she caught a glimpse of his face and noticed his Phillies shirt. Grabbing Sydney's arm, she said, "Oh, there's that man again. The one in the picture." Kate pointed at him.

"Is he here with someone else?" Sydney asked. "Or is he alone again?"

"Looks like he's alone. That's kind of weird, isn't it? Don't people usually come to games with friends or family members?"

"Usually," Sydney agreed.

The man sat down, but Kate kept watching him. A shiver ran down her spine every time she saw the stranger, but she wasn't sure why.

"Looks like there's a family to his right and a young couple on his left. But he's sitting in the same seat as before." She watched him through the binoculars. "He has an MP3 player in his hand again."

"So?" Andrew gave her a curious look. "Lots of people bring MP3 players to the game. What's wrong with that?"

"Something's attached to it." Kate watched him through the binoculars, and then had another brilliant beyond brilliant idea. "See that empty seat in the row in front of him? The one next to the older man with the white hair?"

Andrew looked beyond all of the people seated in front of them until he could clearly see. Then he nodded. "Oh yeah. I see it now. What about it?"

"It's been empty all this time. I don't think anyone is using that seat. So I'm going to go sit in front of our suspect to see what I can see."

"Our *suspect*?" Sydney and Andrew said at the same time.

"What makes that man a suspect?" Andrew asked. "He hasn't even done anything suspicious!"

"Oh, it's just a gut feeling," Kate said, feeling that little shiver again. "I know in my brain that he's up to no good." How she knew, she couldn't say.

"Wow." Andrew shook his head. "I guess I have a lot to learn about solving mysteries. I just thought he was an ordinary fan."

"He probably is." Sydney laughed. "But Kate will figure it out, one way or the other."

"That's why I'm going down there to sit," Kate explained. "If I sit in front of him, I'll hear everything he says. I don't want to falsely accuse him, after all. There are enough rumors flying around."

"Good point." Sydney nodded.

"I brought the perfect thing for looking at things in the row behind me. . . ." Kate reached into her gadget bag and pulled out her large pair of sunglasses.

Andrew looked at her like she was crazy. "Sunglasses? In the stadium?"

"Oh, they're not just sunglasses," she explained. "They've got side mirrors. See right here?" Kate pointed to the tiny mirrors. "When I put these on, I can see what's happening behind me."

"No way." His mouth gaped.

She nodded and handed them to him. He put them on and then whispered, "Hey, the lady behind me is eating nachos. Do you think she'll share? They look great!"

Kate laughed. "You'll have to ask her. Meanwhile, I'm going to go down there. Well, if your mom says it's okay." She turned to Mrs. Smith, explaining her plan. "I promise to stay right there."

"Just be careful, honey. Don't do or say anything to that man if you can help it."

"Oh, trust me. I'm a supersleuth! I won't give myself away." *I hope!*

Kate wiggled through the crowded row of people until she reached the stairs. Then she climbed down one, two, three, four rows. She looked beyond all of the people in that row till she saw the empty seat. Then she whispered a prayer that God would help her with this plan.

Feeling more courageous than before, she eased herself beyond the screaming fans. Just then, one of the players hit a home run. Perfect! With all of the standing and cheering, no one even noticed that she slipped into the seat. She sat and quickly pulled the glasses from her bag. Thankfully, they fit over her regular glasses. As she pressed them into place, she had a clear view of the man behind her. She grabbed her digital recorder and began to whisper into it.

"Male suspect, late twenties. Wearing a Phillies T-shirt. Holding an MP3 player, brand unknown. Has a suspicious look on his face. His gaze keeps shifting. He's not watching the game at all. Must be here for other reasons. Keeps looking at the ground."

Just as she said "looking at the ground," the elderly man with the white hair in the seat next to her gave her a strange look. "Do you mind if I ask what you're doing, kid? You're making me nervous. Whom are you talking to?"

"Oh, I, um. . ." She shrugged. "I'm just taking notes."

"About the game?" His already-wrinkled forehead wrinkled even more. "What are you, a reporter or something? You're a little young to be working for one of the papers. And you're certainly not a TV reporter."

"Well. . ." Kate pulled off the glasses and looked into his eyes. Actually, now that she was writing articles for the blog site about the team, she could *almost* be considered a reporter, right? Still, she didn't feel right saying so. But what could she do to keep the man from asking so many questions?

She pointed at her digital recorder. "I'm just working on a project for a friend. I'm not a real reporter, but I am taking notes. It's a *top secret* project." Kate shrugged and smiled at him, hoping he wouldn't ask anything else.

"Well, would you mind working on it in someone else's seat?" He crossed his arms at his chest and gave her a stern look. "My wife is running late, but when she gets here, she'll want her seat. She'll be mad if I give it to a pip-squeak like you."

What is it with everyone thinking I'm so small? Kate wanted to say, but didn't. Instead, she sighed and muttered, "I'm sorry I bothered you. I'll move."

She started to stand, but all of a sudden the man's mean look faded and a crooked smile took its place. He gave her a sympathetic nod. "Aw, never mind, kid. It'll be awhile before Margaret gets here. She's visiting with the grandkids. So just sit there until she does. And take good notes—for whatever it is you're working on. I'll just sit here and pretend you're some big-name reporter doing a story on the local news or something. You've intrigued me with that top secret stuff."

"Oh, thank you!" Kate could hardly keep from squealing. "Thanks *so* much." She looked down at the field, noticing Tony as he caught a ball in his glove. "My friend thanks you."

"Mm-hmm." He turned his attention back to the game,

but Kate had other things to do. She focused on the mirrors in her glasses and watched in awe as the man behind her punched the buttons on the MP3 player in his hand.

"It's definitely attached to something," she whispered into the digital recorder. "But what? And why?" After a few more minutes of glancing downward, she realized it was a cord of some sort. And it ran all the way down below the seats.

"No way!" He was surely up to something! But in order to know for sure, she'd have to take a closer look.

Kate pulled out her digital camera. How could she take a picture of his MP3 player without him knowing it? And yet she must! She'd never be able to look up that particular model on the Internet unless she got a closer look.

An idea occurred to her quite suddenly. She turned around and looked up three rows to where Sydney sat with Mrs. Smith and Andrew. With a bright smile on her face, she stood to her feet and gave them a big wave, as if she were greeting old friends she hadn't seen in years. The man with the MP3 player looked at her curiously but didn't say anything. Thankfully, Andrew and Sydney waved back, though Mrs. Smith looked a little confused.

Kate lifted her cell phone and pretended to take a picture of them. Just for effect, she hollered out, "Say cheese, Sydney!" then snapped a shot—not of Sydney, but of that *very* interesting-looking MP3 player in the man's hand.

She caught another shot of the man's face. Then she took a picture of Sydney and Andrew, just for fun. The man leaned forward and for the first time Kate could clearly see the cord that ran from the MP3 player underneath the seats. His earphones? Hmm. She'd never seen a cord that long for earphones. *Something very suspicious is going on! But what? And why?*

Just then, the man leaned in her direction and his cap came tumbling off. *Yikes!* Kate used the opportunity to reach down to the ground and snatch it. As she did, she took a good look at the cord. She gasped as she realized it led all the way to the dugout! No, the cord certainly wasn't for earphones. But what in the world was this fellow up to? Why would an ordinary fan do something like this? Goose bumps covered her arms.

"Hey, kid. What are you doing?" an angry voice rang out.

She turned to look at the man in the Phillies shirt, her heart thump-thumping in her chest. "I, um. . ." She held up the cap and smiled innocently. "I thought you might want your cap back. You dropped it." She handed it to him with another big smile.

"Oh." He shoved it on his head and glared at her. "Well, thanks. Now pay attention to the game. You're making me nervous."

She wanted to say, "No, *you're* making *me* nervous," but didn't. No point in making him suspicious.

Kate had just started to breathe a relieved sigh when a shrill voice startled her.

"Excuse me!" Kate looked up to find the owner of the seat staring at her. The older woman had white curls, thin lips, and a mean look on her face. "I think you've got my seat, little lady. Scoot on out of it and go back where you belong."

"Yes, I, well. . ." She swallowed hard then nodded her head. "Your husband said I could. . . Oh, never mind. You're right. So sorry. Have a nice day." As she scooted past the older couple, she hollered out, "Go, Phillies!" then darted back to her seat.

Sydney grabbed her hand as she took her real seat once again. "Oh, I saw the whole thing through the binoculars! Good save! I'm so proud of you. But I was a nervous wreck, Kate. I was praying the whole time."

"Thanks." Kate sighed. "I needed it, trust me. Oh, but, Sydney, I got a couple of great photos. I want to look up the MP3 player on the Internet. I think I know what he's doing with it, but I want to be sure."

"You go, Inspector Gadget!" Sydney giggled. "So what are you thinking? Is it a regular MP3 player that just plays music, or one of those nifty ones you can record with?"

"I'm not sure. I think it does both." She opened the phone and looked at the picture a little more closely. "I'll figure this out; don't worry."

She reached over to turn on her Internet watch. Unfortunately, she couldn't connect with the Internet.

"They must not have wireless access here," she said with a sigh. "I'll have to wait and check it out on our computer at home."

"Aw, don't worry!" Sydney said. "You'll figure it out. I know you will."

"Yeah, but my birthday is Wednesday, and I want to get this case behind me before then," Kate explained. "I don't want to be thinking about solving this mystery on my big day! I want to have fun."

"Oh, we will. . .even if we're still on the case," Sydney said.

"Did I tell you where we're going?" Kate asked. When Sydney shook her head, she continued. "My parents are taking us to the coolest '50s-style soda shop for burgers, fries, and ice cream. Oh, it's the best place in town. The waiters and waitresses are dressed up in '50s costumes and they sing and dance every hour on the hour. We're going to have a blast—but only if I'm not thinking about who's trying to frame Tony Smith. So I don't want to waste even a minute!"

The crowd roared and Sydney rose to her feet, hollering at the top of her lungs. "Woo-hoo! We're not wasting any time at all, Kate. Don't you see? We're at a baseball game in one of the coolest stadiums in the world. Put away those gadgets and enjoy the game. There will be plenty of time for crime solving later!"

With a smile, Kate decided to do just that! She put away her gizmos and turned her attention to the game.

Clues, Clues, and More Clues!

On Monday morning, Kate received a call from Bailey.

"I have a lot of information for your blog site, Kate," Bailey said gleefully. "Hope you're ready for this. I've been working extra hard!"

"Am I ever!" Kate said. "And thanks! Let me get to the computer so I can write all of this down!" She dashed downstairs with Sydney on her heels. Opening a blank screen, she said, "Go ahead, Bailey. I'm ready!"

"Great. Well, let's get started. I wrote down a lot of notes since I went to the library. Hmm, let's see. . ." She paused a moment. "I'll start with this information. The team was founded over a hundred years ago."

"Wow. A hundred years? I didn't even know there was baseball that long ago," Kate said. She couldn't imagine it!

"There was!" Bailey responded. "And Philadelphia had a team! But did you know they weren't always called the Phillies? They were originally called the Quakers."

"Wow. The Quakers? That's interesting. What else?"

"The Phillies are a major league team," Bailey explained, never missing a beat.

"That's good?" Kate asked.

"Yes, Mystery Queen," Bailey said. "They're professionals. And they're also members of the eastern division of the National League."

Kate didn't know what that meant, exactly, but typed it anyway. Maybe Sydney could fill her in later. "What else?"

"The Phillies won the World Series championship in 1980," Bailey continued. "Against Kansas City. They had a video clip of that at the library."

"Wow, a world championship," Kate responded, scribbling down the information. "That's good, right?"

"Yes, my baseball-deprived friend. That's good." Bailey laughed. "They also won the National League East Division in 2007. And in 2008 they changed their uniforms." She went on to explain lots of other things about the team, and before long Kate had tons of information to add to the blog site. Oh, she could hardly wait! It would be the coolest Phillies site ever! One that hundreds—no, *thousands*—of people would want to visit!

Wow! Kate could hardly believe it! She quickly scribbled down the things Bailey told her. *Oh, I hope I'm not missing anything!* She'd never typed so quickly.

"Oh, Bailey, terrific!" Kate said as they finished. "Thank you, big-time! And. . .go Phillies!" For the first time, she really meant those words. It felt good to finally be a fan!

She ended the call with a giggle. Then Sydney called Alex, getting even more information! Afterwards, they signed online and Kate plugged in the information, making the site the best it could be. After that, she tweaked the colors a bit and then wrote an upbeat article about Tony Smith, telling what a great player he was and how much he loved the team. She read through it three times just to make sure it was good. For fun, she even uploaded a couple of cool pictures she'd taken with her camera at that first game, pictures of Tony catching a ball. That should get people interested in the site and in Tony! And it should prove that he was still a great player, despite what people thought about him.

Sydney sat at Kate's side as she worked, offering suggestions and making comments. Finally, Kate added the finishing touches. She sat back in her chair and looked at the blog site one last time. "So what do you think, Sydney?" she asked, staring at it in awe. Her heart thump-thumped with excitement.

"I think it's a-*ma*-zing." Her friend grinned. "I think *you're* amazing. You're not just good with gadgets. You're good with just about everything. This is the coolest blog site I've ever seen, and Phillies fans are going to love it! And I'm pretty sure people from all over the country are going to visit this site and post comments."

Kate practically beamed with joy. It felt good to hear such kind words from her friend. "Hopefully we'll catch whoever is doing this to Mr. Smith, then," she said.

Sydney's expression changed, and for a moment Kate could see the anxiety in her eyes. "Just be prepared, Kate. In order to catch the bad guys, we'll probably have to read some not-so-nice stuff about Tony. Mean stuff, even."

"Yeah, I know." Kate sighed. "But it'll be worth it to find out who's doing this." As she looked at the photos on the site, she remembered something. "Oh, I forgot to upload that one picture I took of that guy's MP3 player. I've got it on my camera, right here."

She grabbed her tiny digital camera once again and transferred the photo of the MP3 player onto the computer so she could enlarge it for a closer look. "All I need is the brand name and the model number. Then I'll be able to track it down. Surely the company that makes them has a Web site. I'm gonna figure this out."

It didn't take long to figure out the MP3 player was called the Audio Wizard by a company called Tekkno-Elekktronix.

"Hmm. Never heard of this brand or model," Kate said. "Just goes to show you I don't know about every gadget! I'll bet my dad's never even heard of this one! Must be new on the market or he would've told me."

"Well, let's find their Web site," Sydney said. "That

would be the best way to get information."

"Probably." After a few minutes of browsing the Web, Kate located the Tekkno-Elekktronix site with a picture of that same MP3 player. She read all of the information on it then looked over at Sydney, stunned.

"This is different from any other audio players I've ever seen," she said, staring at the site. "It's got all sorts of cool capabilities. See this cable?" she pointed at a long black cord in the picture.

Sydney nodded. "What about it?"

"Well, I'm pretty sure it's the same one the man at the game was using. I thought maybe it was an earphone cable at first, but that's not it at all. Look at the end of the cable." She grew more animated with each word. "That's a tiny microphone."

"No way." Sydney leaned closer and gasped. "Oh, you're right! Looks like a clip-on one. Is that what the guy at the game was using? A microphone?"

"Yes." Kate bounced up and down in her seat. "That has to be it! Sydney! I'm really, really sure I know how Mr. Smith's voice ended up on the radio. That man at the stadium has been recording Tony's conversations in the dugout, then using them as voice-overs and pretend interviews for blog sites and radio interviews."

"But that doesn't make sense. Tony wouldn't be saying anything about being unhappy with the team in the dugout." Sydney gave a little shrug. "Just the opposite, in fact. I'm sure when he's with the other players, he's saying nice things."

"Oh, I know. But words can be twisted, you know. Even good words. And before long, rumors can fly. Let me show you how I think he did it." Kate closed out the Web site and opened a software program on the computer. "Check out this software my dad installed. I think you're going to find this interesting."

Sydney shrugged. "What about it?"

"It has voice-editing capabilities."

"Oh?" Sydney still looked confused.

"Yeah, let's try it out. Why don't you say something into the computer's microphone and I'll record you."

Sydney leaned into the little microphone and said, "Okay." After pausing for a minute, she said, "I miss all of my friends from Discovery Lake Camp. Remember when we first met Bailey? A little girl with big ideas! And Alex. . .she knows everything there is to know about Nancy Drew. Good thing we asked her to help us with this case. And Elizabeth. . ." Sydney sighed. "I sure miss Elizabeth, don't you? I don't know anyone who knows as much about the Bible as she does. And I miss McKenzie. She's so smart. She always knows just what to do. I didn't really like all of the food. Some of it was pretty bad, too. But the people were fun."

Kate recorded every word and then played it back. "Okay, sounds great. Now let me try something." She worked with the recording for a few minutes, cutting out some of the words. Then she played it back.

"I sure don't miss my friends at Discovery Lake camp. And I don't like Bailey. Elizabeth was pretty bad, too."

"Whoa." Sydney looked at her, stunned. "Well, that's my voice, all right. But that's not what I said at all."

"Exactly." Kate nodded. "I just took the things you did say and rearranged them to come up with this version."

"Scary!" Sydney's eyes widened. "Very scary!"

"Yes, and I'd be willing to bet that's exactly what the guy at the game did after he recorded Tony Smith's voice. He altered it; then he started the rumors with twisted-up words."

"You're probably right. But it makes me wonder what Tony really said."

"Probably something completely innocent. You can see how easy it is to twist words."

"Yes, I can." Sydney had a worried look on her face. "But why?"

"Good question." Kate shook her head. "If he's a Phillies fan, why would he want to sabotage one of their players?"

"Hmm." Sydney began to pace. "Maybe a news station is paying him to get a juicy story to increase their ratings. You know? Like what happened to Alexis at that nature center with the dinosaurs. The case we called 'Alexis and the Sacramento Surprise.' Maybe he's a reporter or something, just out for a story!"

"Maybe." Kate sighed. "But that angle doesn't make a lot of sense. They have too many big stories right now anyway. Can you think of anything else?"

Sydney's eyes widened. "Ooh! Maybe he's mad because Tony's a shortstop."

"But why?"

"I dunno." Sydney shrugged. "Maybe our bad guy played shortstop in high school and hoped to get drafted to the pros someday. Could be *he* wanted to play for the Phillies, even. You never know. There are probably a lot of bitter wannabe players out there who never got their shot at the pros."

"Maybe." Kate stood and began to pace the room. "Or. . .maybe he's not a Phillies fan at all. Maybe he's a spy for another team. Maybe he's there to bring down the Phillies' morale so they'll lose their games. What do you think of that? Makes perfect sense to me. If you can turn team members against each other, they won't play as well. Before long, they'll start losing games."

"Well, I know I don't perform as well when my spirits are low," Sydney said. "So that makes sense."

"Exactly. So maybe this person is really just trying to get everyone worked up. . .over nothing!"

"I don't know. Maybe." Sydney shrugged. "But one thing is for sure—we're making progress! Before you know it this crime will be solved!"

"Hopefully in time for my birthday," Kate added with a wink. "It's on Wednesday, you know." She wanted to get this case behind them!

"Of course I know!" Sydney laughed. "You've only told me 150 times. You were born on the Fourth of July!"

"My mom says I'm a Yankee Doodle Dandy," Kate said with a grin. "And I love the fact that everyone sets off fireworks on my big day. It's a reminder that God thinks I'm special."

"You *are* special, Kate." Sydney flashed a smile. "But not just on the Fourth of July. You're special every day of the year, I'm so glad God made us friends!"

"Camp Club Girls forever!" Kate shouted.

"Forever and ever!" Sydney echoed.

Just then, Dexter rushed by and shouted, "Boys rule, girls drool!"

Kate laughed. "It's the other way around, silly. Girls rule, *boys* drool."

"Oh." He grabbed his robotic car and put it down on the floor, making it spin in circles. Biscuit, who was trailing along behind the girls, began to bark and run in circles behind the car. Pretty soon he gave up and dropped onto the floor panting.

Kate laughed. "Silly dog. When will you ever learn?"

In some ways, watching Biscuit chase that car was a little like solving a case. If you weren't careful, before long you were just going in circles, getting nowhere. And it could wear you out, too!

Dexter scooped up the car in his hand and headed off into the other room. "I told you. . .boys are the best. I can always fool Biscuit. Some crime solver he is! And you girls think you're the best, but boys really are!" He walked off, muttering something about how girls weren't as smart as boys.

"He doesn't know how great the Camp Club Girls are, or he wouldn't be saying that," Sydney said, turning Kate's way. "But we'll forgive him. He's just a kid."

"Hey, I'm no kid!" Dex's voice rang out from the next room. "I'm almost nine! That's practically a teenager."

Both of the girls laughed.

"I can hardly remember what life was like when I was nine," Sydney said with a wink. "That was years ago!"

"And now that I'm almost twelve, nine seems *forever* ago!" Kate added. "A million jillion years, even."

Thinking of turning twelve reminded her of her birthday party. Thinking of her birthday party reminded her that they had to solve the case in just two days! Thinking about solving the case in such a short amount of time reminded her that they really, really needed to get to work.

"C'mon, Sydney!" she said, grabbing her friend's hand. "Let's send another e-mail to the Camp Club Girls! We need them now more than ever!"

SWAT-bot to the Rescue!

The following morning, Kate received a call from Andrew. He sounded out of breath and very upset. In fact, she could hardly understand his words.

"K–Kate! Something terrible has happened!"

For a second, she thought he might start to cry. Kate sat straight up in the bed, clutching the phone to her ear as she asked, "What? What happened, Andrew? Tell me!"

"S–someone tried to b–break into our house last night. Our alarm went off. Thank goodness the person took off. Nothing was stolen, so that's good. But it was awful!"

"Ooh!" Kate shivered just thinking about it. "How scary! Did you wake up? Did you see him? What did he look like? Did the police come? Is your dad upset? What about your mom? How is she doing? Do we need to come over and help? Should I wake up my parents? What can I do?"

"Slow down, slow down. . . ." Andrew groaned. "You always move too fast for me, Kate. I can never keep up."

"Sorry." She drew in a deep breath and waited a second.

"But I'm just so upset, Andrew! This is awful!"

Just then, Sydney woke up and popped up in the bed. "What happened?" she asked, rubbing her eyes. "Something with Andrew?"

Kate nodded. She put her hand over the phone and whispered, "Yes. Someone tried to break into the Smiths' house last night. A burglar! Isn't that awful?"

Sydney's eyes grew wider and wider. "Did he steal anything?"

"No." Kate shook her head. "And everyone's safe." She turned her attention back to her friend on the phone. "Andrew, I'm going to talk to my dad. Remember I told you about SWAT-bot—the little security robot he created? The one that just got patented?"

"Sure. But what does that have to do with anything?"

"Hang on and I'll explain. See, my dad is working on a second one. . .a more advanced version. I'll bet he will loan it to you if I ask. Would you like me to ask?"

"Would I! I'd feel so much safer if I knew SWAT-bot was on the job." Andrew sounded relieved, and Kate was happy to help. She felt sure her father would agree.

"Here's the really cool part," Kate said. "If anyone tries to break in again, SWAT-bot will call the police right away. He's programmed to do that. He'll recognize who belongs in the house and who doesn't. My dad can explain how all of that works. But here's the neatest thing of all—I know you won't believe this! He'll also take pictures and video without the person knowing. That's something ordinary alarm systems don't do. He also records voices and turns them into digital files that can be played back later. So if a crime is committed, he's a witness!"

"But what if the bad guys just steal him? He's really small, right? If they do that, the police won't know what to do or who took him."

"Wrong!" Kate said with glee. "If the burglar steals SWAT-bot, his GPS tracking device will lead the police right to the criminals and they won't even know they're being followed! Isn't that the coolest thing? He's a surefire security-bot!" She started to say how proud she was of her dad for inventing it, but Andrew interrupted her.

"That's cooler than all of your other devices put together." He paused. "Just let me know what your dad says, okay? I'm going to tell my parents right now. And thanks, Kate. I don't know what we'd do without you. I really mean that."

"Oh, I'm happy to help!"

As she finished, Sydney looked at her curiously. "We're getting closer to figuring this out, aren't we? I can feel it! We'll solve this case in no time."

"With God's help." Kate paused a moment and said, "So I guess we'd better ask Him for His help, because I sure can't do this on my own!" She took Sydney's hands in hers and they bowed their heads.

"Lord, it's me, Kate Oliver. Again. I know You know who I am because the Bible says You even know how many hairs are on my head. That's a lot more than I know, Lord."

Sydney chuckled but didn't say anything.

"Anyway, Lord, we really need Your help right now!" Kate continued. "We're on a big case and we don't have answers. But You do! We ask You to protect the Smith family and lift their spirits. And help us find whoever is doing this so everyone can see how great and mighty You are. In Jesus' name. . ."

"Amen!" She and Sydney shouted together.

Kate swung her legs over the side of the bed. "We have work to do, Sydney! I'd be willing to bet that would-be burglar is somehow connected to that guy at the stadium, but we have to prove it! I'm putting SWAT-bot to work!"

"Let's do it!"

Minutes later, Kate and Sydney bounded down the stairs. As always, she nearly tripped over her brother, who played with his electronic cars. "Dex, watch what you're doing! Playing with your cars on the stairs is dangerous."

He scooted over to let them go by, mumbling, "Boys rule, girls drool."

Kate just rolled her eyes. She ran into the kitchen, where her father was at the breakfast table reading the paper. He looked up as she came racing in.

"Dad, I need to borrow the newer, more advanced SWAT-bot. Is he ready to help solve a crime?"

"Solve a crime?" He put the paper down and gave her a curious look. "What are you talking about, honey? Why do you need SWAT-bot again?"

She quickly told him what had happened at Andrew's house and her father flew into action. He went down into the basement and came up with the security robot in his hands. "I'm not quite done tweaking him, so his photo abilities might be limited. But I think the video recorder works. And I checked the GPS tracking device yesterday, so it's working fine."

Kate patted the little robot on the head. "Work hard, SWAT-bot, and maybe you'll be famous someday! You'll get your picture in the paper!"

"Do you want me to drive you girls to the Smiths' house?" Kate's dad asked.

"Yes, please!" Kate jumped up and down, ready to roll!

Sydney grinned. "I'm gonna get to see Tony Smith's house? How cool is that! But do we have time for me to run first? I haven't exercised in days and I'm starting to feel flabby."

"Flabby?" Kate looked at her and laughed. "You're all muscle."

"It'll take me a few minutes to get ready," Kate's father said. "So go for a run, Sydney. But be back as soon as you can."

About ten minutes later, with Sydney a little out of breath, everyone climbed into the family van and Kate's dad drove them to the Smiths' beautiful two-story home with blue shutters. She had only been to Andrew's house a couple of times before, but never with Sydney. Her friend seemed overjoyed at the idea of going to a pro ballplayer's house.

When they arrived, Mr. and Mrs. Smith were still talking to the police. Mrs. Smith even had tears in her eyes. And Tony's fists were clenched, like he was angry. But who could blame them? Kate would be upset if someone broke into her house, too!

They invited Kate, her dad, and Sydney inside and then continued talking to the officer, who took notes of everything they said. He left after a few minutes, promising to do all he could to help. Kate wondered what it would be like to be a police officer. Surely his crime solving abilities were even better than those of the Camp Club Girls!

As soon as the policeman left, Kate's dad went back out to the van and brought SWAT-bot into the house. "I want to loan you a new security device," he explained. "I think he's going to come in handy."

"*He*?" Tony's eyes grew wide. "Is this a robot? I've never seen anything like this little guy before. I've heard about them, of course, but never seen one."

"He's not on the market yet," Kate's dad explained. "But

hopefully he will be before long. This is SWAT-bot, and he'll help protect your home."

"Wow." Tony stared at the little robot. "That's pretty amazing. Is it complicated to use?"

"It's not as difficult as it looks," Kate's dad explained. "In fact, he's pretty simple to operate. And you can check on your house no matter where you are. Just call this number"—he handed him a piece of paper with a number on it—"and SWAT-bot will report any suspicious activities."

"That's the coolest thing I've ever heard," Tony said with a nod. "And a lot better than our current security system."

"That's why my dad got a patent for SWAT-bot," Kate said, beaming with pride. "He's going to be super famous."

"Hardly." Her dad laughed. "And I have no interest in being famous, for that matter. But if he helps keep people safe, then I'm a happy camper."

Hearing the words "happy camper" made Kate think of the Camp Club Girls. She would send them an e-mail to update them on the case, especially the part about Andrew's house getting broken into. Surely Elizabeth would put her prayer warriors to work! And McKenzie would probably be full of great ideas. So would the other girls.

Kate's dad continued showing Tony how to use the little security robot and said, "If you have any questions, you can always call me."

"I can't thank you enough." Tony walked with them to

the door, but Kate could tell Sydney didn't want to leave. She paused at the door of the library—the room nearest the front of the house—with her mouth hanging open.

"Oh my goodness!" She pointed at the awards and plaques on the wall, turning in a slow circle to see them all. "Is all of this yours, Mr. Smith?"

"Yes." He nodded but looked a little embarrassed. "But I told you girls to call me Tony. Everyone does."

"Okay. Tony." Sydney looked at him and beamed. "C–can I look at some of these?"

"Of course." He flipped on the light in the library and led the way inside.

Kate stared at the walls filled with framed certificates, plaques, and awards. She'd never seen so many things of honor in one place before! Why, Mr. Smith must be a real superstar. Even her dad looked impressed, and he didn't care much about sports!

Tony led them around the room and showed them all of his awards. He explained each one. Sydney's eyes looked like they might just pop out of her head!

"This just makes me want to play ball!" she said. "Oh, I wish I could get out on that field and hit a homer for the Phillies!"

Kate giggled, watching her friend. What fun this must be for a sports nut like Sydney! This was probably almost as exciting to her as solving a case! At least, it seemed that way.

As he finished up the tour, Mr. Smith reached for a baseball and tossed it into the air. "I have quite a few of these signed baseballs if you girls want one." His expression grew sad. "Not many fans are asking for them these days." He set it on the desk with a sigh.

"Are you kidding? I'll take one!" Sydney practically jumped up and down. "Thank you, Mr. Smith. . .er, Tony. This is the best gift I've ever received."

"No problem! Happy to do it."

Kate was so thrilled for her friend. If anyone deserved a special gift, it was Sydney. Meeting Mr. Smith face-to-face was probably one of the coolest things that could've happened to her. And to get a signed baseball made it even better!

Tony led them back into the big foyer, and Kate could tell they were about to leave. She looked up at Mr. Smith, wanting to take care of one more piece of business. "Oh, while I'm here, is there some way to find out the name and maybe even the address of someone who has season tickets to the Phillies games?"

"Hmm." Tony's brow wrinkled. "Well, I might be able to contact a friend of mine who works up at the box office. But why?"

"Well. . ." She hesitated to tell him, afraid he might think she was crazy. "I, um. . ."

"Go ahead and tell me, Kate," he said, looking

concerned. "Maybe I can help you if I know more."

"Okay." She exhaled loudly. "I saw a man at the stadium. . .and I can't be sure, but I think maybe he's the same man who tried to break into your house."

"What?" Tony looked tense. "What makes you say that?"

Kate quickly explained about the man at the stadium and his suspicious actions. When she told Tony about the MP3 player and the cord attached to it, he looked stunned.

"Are you saying someone's been taping my voice without my knowledge?"

"Maybe," Kate said. "At least, that's what I suspect. And I think he's been working hard to make you look bad, taking your words and twisting them up to make it sound like you don't like the team."

"Whoa!" Tony said. "That's scary."

"Yes, but it makes perfect sense," Kate's father said. "He must've edited your words and used them against you."

"That's awful," Mrs. Smith said, fanning herself. "Who would do such a terrible thing. . .and why?" For a minute, she looked like she might cry again. Kate almost felt like crying herself!

"That's what I'm trying to figure out," she explained. "And you have nothing to worry about! Sydney and I are on the case! And the rest of the Camp Club Girls are helping us!" She told them all about McKenzie, Alex, Elizabeth, and Bailey. Mr. and Mrs. Smith looked very impressed.

117

"Well, with so many supersleuths on the job, I'm sure we'll catch this bad guy in no time," Tony said. "And in the meantime, I'll contact my friend at the stadium box office. Maybe he'll tell me who sits in that seat—especially if he knows it's related to the break-in of my home. I'll have to share anything I learn with the police, of course."

"Of course!" she agreed.

Mr. Smith said good-bye to Kate's dad and waved to both of the girls as they walked toward the car. "I can't thank you enough!" he hollered from the front door. "And when you catch the person who's doing this, I'll treat you to something really special! Just wait and see!"

"Something special?" Sydney gasped then whispered to Kate, "What do you think he means?" After a second of staring into space, she squealed, "Oh! Maybe he'll give us a tour of the stadium!"

"Or maybe he'll ask us to sing the national anthem before a big game." Kate giggled. "That would be hysterical. Have you ever heard me sing before?"

Sydney laughed. "Yeah. I remember hearing you at camp. You weren't so bad."

"I wasn't so *good*, either." Kate giggled again. "But that's okay. Whatever Mr. Smith has in mind will be awesome. But first"—she looked back toward his house as he closed the door—"first we have to solve this case!"

Blogging for Clues

When Kate and Sydney arrived back home, they decided it was time to check out their new blog site to see if anyone had visited or left comments. Kate was thrilled to see that several of the Camp Club Girls and their friends had posted enthusiastic notes about Tony Smith. She glanced over the first few, impressed by how much the girls seemed to know about the Phillies.

Am I the only one who knows nothing about baseball? Hmm.

She would really have to do something about that. Maybe by the end of all this, she'd be the biggest Phillies fan ever!

"Hey, Sydney," Kate said, waving her hand. "Come on over and check this out."

Sydney drew near and whistled as Kate scrolled down, down, down, showing her the comments on their site. "Wow! Go, Camp Club Girls!"

"Looks like they got their friends and even some of their

family members to post, too." Kate scrolled down through all of the comments, smiling as she read most of them. However, she soon stumbled across one that didn't sound so nice, one she felt sure the girls hadn't written.

"Oh, look here, Sydney." She pointed at the screen. "This lady—I guess she's a lady—her screen name is PhiladelphiaLadyBug—is really mad at Tony Smith. She said some ugly things. I don't think she likes him very much!"

Sydney drew near and they both read the comment.

Go ahead and write your mushy articles about Tony Smith. I won't be reading them. He is a traitor to the team. I've lived in Philadelphia all of my life and we've never had a team member I've been ashamed of until now. He needs to go back to wherever he came from—and the sooner, the better!

"Wow." Kate felt a little mad as she read the note. "That's totally mean. I understand people getting upset— after all, they've been reading all of those other blog sites and listening to that radio interview—but that was really a rude thing to say."

Thankfully, the next few comments Kate read were nice. Then she stumbled across a really, really bad one! "Oh my. This one is *awful*." She read it from start to finish, goose bumps working their way down her arms.

> *I don't know who started this site or why, but*
> *you will be stopped. Tony Smith is not the*
> *hero you've painted him to be. In fact, he is*
> *just the opposite. Read the Web. Listen to the*
> *radio. Hear what the fans and other players*
> *have to say. Then you'll stop writing articles*
> *like this. And if you DON'T...*

"If we don't?" Kate shivered a bit. "Then what?"

"Ooh, this is awful!" Sydney said. "Who does he think he is? And what is he going to do to us if we keep this blog site going? Sounds like a threat."

"It does sound like a threat. But we don't even know it's a he," Kate said. "The screen name just says PhilliesFan29."

She shook her head, a scary feeling gripping her. "Hey, didn't we see that name on one of those other blog sites we visited the other day? Seems like we did."

"Hmm." Sydney looked at it closely. "PhilliesFan29. That *does* sound familiar."

Kate quickly did a search and found several sites with the name PhilliesFan29 on them. In every case, the comments were about Tony and were very mean! She read through every one and then kept searching, searching, searching for that original site—the one they'd seen that first day. The one Andrew had told them about. Finally she found it!

"Look, Sydney! This site belongs to that man, PhilliesFan29. His whole Web site is mostly just mean stuff he wrote about Tony. And now it looks like he's been traveling around the Web, finding every site that says anything good about Tony, and leaving ugly comments."

"The puzzle pieces are starting to come together," Sydney agreed. "PhillesFan29 is our bad guy, isn't he? He's the one who started all of the rumors about Tony, and now he's really mad because we've been saying nice things about him. I guess that got this guy all worked up." She gripped her hands together. "But what do you think he'll do? I don't like to be threatened."

"Aw, don't worry. The worst he can do is hack our site," Kate explained.

"Hack our site?" Sydney looked confused.

"Rewrite it, replacing our words with his. Or remove it from the Web altogether." She flashed a confident smile. "But don't worry. I'll take care of that. I'll set up the site so, as the administrator, I have to approve whatever anyone wants to post before it's put online. That should stop him." She shook her head. "I just wish I knew who this guy was and why he would care so much about Tony Smith, of all people."

"Yeah, it's obvious he's not really after us. He's after

Tony," Sydney agreed. "But why? That's the part we still have to figure out!"

"Maybe we need to dig a little deeper," Kate said. "Keep searching the Web for more signs of PhilliesFan29. If we do, we might learn more."

Sydney stood and began to do her stretches.

"What are you doing?" Kate asked.

"I always exercise when I'm nervous," she explained.

"That's funny." Kate laughed. "I always eat—Twinkies, mostly. And Ding Dongs."

Sydney started doing jumping jacks, and after a couple of minutes Kate's mother stuck her head in the door. "Everything okay?" She looked at Sydney and smiled. "Ah, that explains it! I felt the floor shaking and wondered what it was."

"Oh, sorry!" Sydney stopped, looking a little embarrassed.

"No, go right ahead. I'm just happy to know everything's okay." She disappeared from view and Sydney dropped to the floor and started her sit-up routine.

Kate continued to browse the Web. After a little more searching, she stumbled across a personal blog site that belonged to PhilliesFan29. She read a few words, then gasped.

"Look, Sydney! His real name is J. Kenner. Wish I knew what the *J* stands for. Oh, and look. There's even a picture of him. He's not very old, maybe late twenties. I guess the 29 in his name means he's twenty-nine years old. She stared at the photograph of the man, and a cold chill wriggled its way over her. "Ooh! Sydney!"

"What?"

"It's that man."

"*That* man? *What* man?" Sydney leaned in to have a closer look. "Who are you talking about?"

"Oh my goodness!" Kate got up and grabbed her digital camera, opening it to the picture of the man at the stadium. "This is the same man, right? The one with the MP3 player. He's wearing a different shirt and his hair is a little darker now, but I'm really, really sure it's the same guy. No doubt about it!"

"Hmm, I'm not completely sure." Sydney turned the camera to get a closer look. "It *could* be him."

"No *could be* about it. This *is* him! The guy at the stadium is J. Kenner!" Her excitement grew as she spoke. "Watch and see! Tony's going to talk to his friend at the box office and they're going to confirm it. I'd bet my hat on it!"

"Do you own a hat?" Sydney asked and then laughed. "But seriously. . .why would this guy go to all of this trouble to hurt a Phillies shortstop? It still doesn't make any sense."

"Yeah. Why pick on Tony Smith?" Kate added. "What did he ever do to J. Kenner, after all?" She racked her brain, trying to come up with something, but nothing made sense. "Maybe they were college roommates or something. Maybe. . ." She paused as an idea struck. "Maybe J. Kenner was jilted in love. Maybe Tony's wife used to be J. Kenner's girlfriend or something like that."

"You've watched too much TV." Sydney laughed and then began to pace the room. "I've seen a lot of strange stuff in my life, you know. Stranger than TV. I live in DC, after all," she said. "And being so near the White House, I hear about lots of crazy things. People just do random, nutty stuff sometimes. Maybe this J. Kenner guy was a jilted T-ball player as a kid. You never know what makes some people snap. One thing's for sure—he has to be stopped."

"Should we go to the police?" Kate asked.

"I'm not sure we have enough evidence," Sydney said. "We need proof that he's the one who recorded Tony's voice and changed it. That means. . ."

Kate gasped. "Are you saying we need to get his MP3 player? I wouldn't feel right taking it, even if he is a criminal. That would be stealing, wouldn't it?"

"Well, I was thinking of *borrowing* it," Sydney explained with a twinkle in her eye. "Not keeping it for long, anyway. Do you think Biscuit might be able to help us get the MP3 player just long enough to pull the audio files from it? He's so good at helping with things like that."

As soon as Biscuit heard his name, he joined them at the computer, whimpering. Kate reached down with her free hand and scratched him behind the ears. "Do you miss us, boy?" She gave him a tender look. "You're used to helping, aren't you? But we can't take you into the stadium, now can we?" She looked at Sydney. "So how could we do it?"

His tail wagged merrily as if he were saying, *"I'd do it if I could."*

"I guess you're right," Sydney said finally. "There's really no way to sneak a dog into Citizens Bank Park, right? They only allow service dogs."

"Service dogs? You mean, like, dogs that belong to people in the army and marines?" Kate asked.

Sydney laughed. "No, silly. I mean service dogs. The ones who travel with handicapped people. But if you don't like the idea of actually getting our hands on the MP3 player, maybe we can find a copy of the audio recording online, if that's possible. That might work just as well."

"Oh, great idea! And my dad's voice-editing software might help us tell where the words were changed. I hope so, anyway."

She quickly typed the words "Tony Smith audio clip" into her search engine. It took some browsing, but eventually they found the radio interview online.

"I feel like we've hit the jackpot," Kate whispered. "This is a gold mine!"

"Well, we prayed. . .and God answered," Sydney said. "Why are we surprised?"

"I guess I shouldn't be, but I am." Kate looked at her friend in awe. "Oh, Sydney, sometimes I just need bigger faith. I need to know that God is going to do what He says He's going to do!"

"Well, this whole thing has been a real faith-builder, hasn't it?" Sydney smiled. "And you know what? Before we do one more thing, before we even listen to that audio clip, I think we need to stop and thank God. We wouldn't know any of this without Him!"

"You're so right!" Kate agreed.

The two girls bowed their heads, and with a voice as clear as crystal, Kate began to pray—thanking God for all He'd done to help them track down the man who had hurt Tony Smith. On and on she went, telling the Lord just how grateful they were!

Then, with a heart filled to overflowing with joy, she turned back to her friend. "Tomorrow's my birthday!" she said, flashing her brightest smile. "And I suddenly feel like celebrating!"

CHAPTER 13

Born on the Fourth of July!

On the morning of Kate's twelfth birthday, she awoke with a smile on her face. "I can't believe it! I'm twelve! Twelve! Almost a teenager!"

She thought about all that had happened over the past week and a half. In that short amount of time, her father had received a patent for SWAT-bot. Sydney had come for a visit. And they'd almost solved a major mystery.

Of course, they still had to track down J. Kenner, but that part she would leave to the police. She'd done a lot already, after all! She had started a blog site, investigated a suspect at the stadium, and figured out the whole PhilliesFan29 angle. Almost, anyway. There was still that one little matter of learning his first name, but that would come. . .in time!

And of course, she still needed to tell her father everything she and Sydney had discovered so that he could contact the proper authorities. They would need all of the correct information to track down the bad guy, and she was happy to share what she'd learned!

However, she would have to do all of that later. Right now, there were important things to do—like celebrating her birthday!

Kate sprang out of bed and pulled the covers off of Sydney. "Wake up! Wake up! This is my big day!"

"Your big day?" Sydney groaned. "What do you mean?"

"Well, for one thing, it's my birthday," Kate said.

"I know, I know. You've told me a thousand times. Happy birthday, Kate!"

"Thank you!" She giggled. "But there's something else. Something I've been dying to tell you. It's a project my dad and I have been working on in the basement for months! A huge secret! I wasn't going to tell anyone until we worked out all of the kinks, but it's my birthday, so I feel like telling you now."

"What is it?" Sydney's nose wrinkled. "What sort of secrets have you been keeping, Kate Oliver? Better tell me. . .quick!"

Kate giggled. "I *have* been keeping secrets, but they're good ones! Instead of telling you, it might be easier to show you." She tugged on Sydney's arm until her friend sat up in the bed.

"Okay, okay!" Sydney laughed. "I guess you're in a hurry, so I'll do my exercises later."

"Don't worry about that," Kate said. "I have just the

thing to help get you moving. Trust me!"

Kate practically pulled Sydney from the bed. Seconds later, the two sprinted down the stairs, and then down the next set of stairs to the basement. Biscuit followed, almost slipping on the bottom step. "Careful, boy!" Kate called out. She turned on the light and Sydney gasped.

"Kate! I've never seen so much stuff! What is all of this?"

"My dad's inventions, remember? I told you! Kind of like *Honey, I Shrunk the Kids*."

"Oh yeah." Sydney looked around with a dazed expression on her face.

"It's an electronic wonderland down here," Kate explained. "Better than an amusement park, and all original stuff!"

"No kidding." Sydney squinted, looking beyond the bright light. "So what am I supposed to be looking at? What's the big surprise?"

"It's right here." She pointed with great joy at the robotic brace she and her father had been working on for children with muscular dystrophy. Picking it up, she explained, "See, it's a brace. Kids who have muscular problems have a hard time performing everyday tasks with their hands."

"Why?" Sydney asked, reaching to hold the brace. She looked it over carefully.

"Well, their upper arms don't work very well," Kate said. "That's why Dad and I created Robo-Brace."

"Robo-Brace?" Sydney echoed.

"Yes, well, it's a brace to help kids with their movement. When they strap this on"—she demonstrated, putting it on her arm—"they have more arm strength and flexibility. It helps them lift things, too." She demonstrated, and Biscuit began to bark and then jump up and down.

"Seriously?" Sydney stared at her, amazed. "Kate, this is one of the coolest things I've ever seen. When are you going to start manufacturing them for the kids with muscular dystrophy?"

"We need to do a lot more work before we'll be ready for that. But I've been working on this idea ever since I heard Andrew's dad was a spokesman for the Muscular Dystrophy Foundation. I wanted to surprise him." She frowned. "And then when I heard they didn't want him for their spokesperson anymore, it broke my heart! We've been working so hard on this secret project!"

"Let me try it!"

"Sure!" Kate helped Sydney strap on the brace, and before long Sydney was moving her arms up, down, and all around.

"Wow, this is giving me quite a workout," Sydney said. "I can feel it in my upper arms and my shoulders."

"Which is exactly where people with muscular dystrophy are weak," Kate explained. "So now you get it!"

"I do!" Sydney giggled. "You're a genius. But what about

Tony Smith? He doesn't even know about all of this? He hasn't seen Robo-Brace?"

"No, never." Kate shrugged. "We were waiting. There's just been too much going on. I didn't want to bother him during that whole rumors fiasco."

"Well, I hope you're able to show him soon!"

"I plan on it," Kate said. She glanced at her watch and then sprang into action. "But first I have to go to a super-fantabulous birthday party!"

Later that afternoon, Kate's parents took the girls, Dexter, and Andrew to Ice De-Lights, a local '50s-style soda shop that specialized in birthday parties. They ordered burgers and fries for everyone, along with a beautiful ice cream cake that read HAPPY BIRTHDAY, INSPECTOR GADGET! Kate laughed when she read it.

They hadn't been there very long when a familiar '50s song started playing. All of the waiters and waitresses gathered in a long line across the front of the restaurant and did a funny little dance. Kate couldn't stop laughing as she watched them. Then—horror of horrors!—one of the waiters asked her to join them because it was her birthday. How embarrassing! She wanted to crawl under one of the tables or run out the door. Instead, she gave it her best effort. Not that she could dance very well, but she tried!

After that, Kate just relaxed and had a great time,

completely forgetting about J. Kenner or anything having to do with Tony Smith. That was, until her dad's phone rang. She could tell it was serious by the expression on his face as he talked.

"What's that?" he asked. "Are you sure?" His eyes grew very, very wide as he listened to the response from the other end of the line.

"What is it, Dad?" Kate asked, looking at her father. "What's happened?"

Kate's father ended the call and looked at all of them. "Well, that was fascinating. Andrew's dad was calling with some very interesting news."

"Interesting news?" Kate bounced up and down, more curious than ever. "Tell us, please!" she chanted. "Oh, Dad, tell us what he said!"

"Yes, please, Mr. Oliver!" Andrew added, his eyes now bugging. "Tell us!"

Kate felt sure she would burst with excitement! What, oh what, had happened?

CHAPTER 14

The Plot Thickens!

Kate could hardly contain her excitement. "What did Mr. Smith say, Dad? What did he say?"

Her father clasped his hands together and smiled. "He found out the name of the man at the stadium—the one you told us about, Kate, in that seat number you wrote down. His name is James Kenner!"

"James Kenner!" Sydney and Kate stared at each other in disbelief. "Wow, I *knew* it," Kate said. "We were right about the Kenner part. And *J* is for James."

"That's just amazing," Sydney added.

"Wait. . . ." Kate's father looked confused. "You mean you girls already knew the man's name?"

"We weren't sure, but I found a blogger online with the last name Kenner," Kate explained. "He was saying lots of bad stuff about Mr. Smith. So I just put two and two together. . . ." She shrugged. "I wanted to talk to you about it this morning, but I got so busy in the basement I almost forgot!"

"Well, speaking of busy, Tony and his wife want us to meet them at their house so we can tell the police everything we know." He winked at Kate. "Do you mind interrupting your birthday party to wrap up this case? After eating the ice cream cake, I mean."

"Mind? Of course not!"

"Well, let's get this show on the road, then," Andrew said. He stood and began to sing "Happy Birthday" to Kate. She felt her cheeks grow warm with embarrassment. First the silly dance and now this? Nothing like being put on the spot in front of a whole restaurant full of people! Kate knew her friend Bailey, one of the Camp Club Girls, would love that kind of attention, but Kate usually didn't like to be noticed so much.

After the singing, Kate blew out the twelve candles on the cake, and her mother sliced it into thick pieces. She could see the yummy strawberry ice cream and chocolate cake layers as her mother laid the pieces on plates.

"Open your presents while I'm serving the cake, honey," her mother said.

First she opened the gift from her parents. Ripping the paper was always such fun! When she got the package open, Kate stared at the red Phillies T-shirt. "Oh, how funny!"

"Well, we figured it was time to start supporting our team," her father said with a wink. "But we have something else for you, too."

Kate opened the second package, stunned to see a necklace with the words INSPECTOR GADGET on it in little red ruby chips, the July birthstone. She stared at her mom and dad, feeling the sting of tears in her eyes. "Oh, Mom! Dad! This is the greatest! Thank you so much!"

Sydney helped her put it on, and then she opened up a small package from Andrew. He watched her carefully. "I really hope you like this," he said. "I bought it just for you."

"Thanks!" She ripped the paper off of the gift and gasped when she saw the tiny electronic baseball game inside. "Andrew, how funny!" She laughed until her sides hurt. "This is great! I can't believe you did this."

"Well, I know how much you like electronics," he said with a nod. "And I know how much you want to learn about baseball, so I figured it was the perfect gift."

"It is!"

Next she opened the present from Sydney. "Sorry, but I didn't have much time to get you anything because I left DC so quickly." Sydney shrugged. "I hope you like it."

Kate stared at the framed photograph of the Camp Club Girls and a lump rose in her throat. "Oh, it's perfect! But I don't remember taking this picture."

"It was right after we found Biscuit." Sydney pointed. "See how scraggly he looks?"

"Oh yes. He does!" Kate looked a little closer. "And he

has put on a few pounds since coming to live with us. I didn't realize until now!"

Her life had changed so much since then. Still, as she stared into the faces of her friends—McKenzie, Alex, Bailey, Elizabeth, and Sydney, she had to smile. What fun they'd had solving that very first case.

Thinking about that first case got her to thinking about the second. And the third. And before long, she was bouncing up and down in her seat, ready to go. But how could she leave without eating cake? No way!

Her mother set a piece of birthday cake in front of her and she licked her lips. "This looks so good!" Kate jabbed her fork into the yummy cold cake. She took a big bite. Then another. Then another. After a few seconds, she grabbed her head. "Ow! Ow!"

"What's wrong?" Her mother looked her way.

"Brain freeze," she said.

"Ah. I get that all the time when I eat ice cream too fast," Andrew said. "Just slow down, Kate."

Slow down? Slow down? Who has time to slow down? She wanted to eat a second piece before going over to the Smiths' house, and she had to do that in a hurry.

As soon as they finished the ice cream cake, Kate grabbed her presents and headed to the van. Her father drove them to the Smiths' house in a hurry. When they arrived, the home was surrounded by police.

"Oh no!" As Kate climbed out of the van, her heart began to beat double-time as she imagined what had happened. She followed Andrew as he ran toward his parents.

"What's going on?" he hollered as they drew near.

"Yes, what's happened?" Kate echoed.

"Oh, it was terrible," Mrs. Smith said, holding her hands to her heart. "We came home from the stadium to get a bite to eat and saw that the front door had been shoved in. The alarm was going off, so I knew the police were on their way, but I was scared to go inside. Your father was brave. He went in."

"Was it James Kenner?" Kate asked, feeling jittery.

"We don't know," Mr. Smith said, shaking his head. "I went inside and checked out the place. Whoever it was tore up my office and stole some of my awards."

"Oh no!" Kate gasped. Sydney looked as if she were going to throw up.

"There's worse news." Mr. Smith looked in Kate's father's direction. "They stole SWAT-bot, too."

"Stole SWAT-bot?" Sydney groaned. "Oh no!"

"Don't worry! Whoever took him won't get away for long!" Kate's dad reached for his cell phone and punched in a telephone number. Within seconds, the GPS tracking system inside of SWAT-bot gave him the robot's exact location. "They're at the corner of Cottonwood and Denning Streets," he hollered. "We have to tell the police."

Kate could hardly contain her excitement! "Oh, Dad! I'm so glad you invented SWAT-bot and gave him so many cool features! You're brilliant!"

Seconds later, a policeman exited the house and listened to their excited tale. He ran for his patrol car and headed off with his sirens blaring. Kate knew he was on his way to the corner of Cottonwood and Denning. She jumped up and down. Oh, how she wanted to get into the patrol car and help the officer!

"Why, oh why, am I only twelve?" she asked, pacing up and down the front sidewalk. "I wanted to be the one to track him down!"

"Well, you did!" Sydney said. "It was your idea to bring SWAT-bot here, wasn't it? And it was also your idea to observe the man at the stadium in the first place. You knew in your gut he was the right guy."

"And I'd be willing to bet the man who stole SWAT-bot is named James Kenner," Kate said with a sigh.

"Otherwise known as PhilliesFan29," Sydney added.

"Some fan! He's nothing but trouble!"

Several minutes later, Tony received a call from the police, telling him they had the man in custody.

"Wow, that was fast!" Kate grew more excited by the minute. "So what's his name? Were we right? Did we figure it out?"

Tony gave her a wink. "What do you think?"

"James Kenner!" Kate, Sydney, and Andrew hollered together.

Tony nodded. "You've got it. Same guy! And that Kenner fellow has a lot of explaining to do."

"Like why he caused so much trouble for you," Mrs. Smith said, giving her husband a warm embrace.

"And why he broke into our house," Mr. Smith added. "I wonder what he was looking for."

"Maybe he wanted to sell your awards to make it look like you didn't care about them," Sydney suggested. "Probably on eBay or something like that."

"That's a good idea," Tony said. "You're a good guesser, Sydney."

Her cheeks turned pink and she looked a little embarrassed, but she said a quiet "Thank you."

"Kenner will never get the chance to sell or destroy any of your things now!" Kate's father explained. "The police caught him right away."

"Thanks to SWAT-bot!" everyone said in unison.

"And thanks to the Camp Club Girls!" Tony added with a twinkle in his eye.

"Maybe things will go back to normal now," Mrs. Smith said with a nod. "That's my prayer."

"Yes, I hope so, too." Tony's face beamed with joy. "I love playing for the Phillies. In fact, I don't know when I've loved the game of baseball more. And now that this episode is behind me, things are going to get even better."

"Yes, as soon as the evening news breaks the story about James Kenner, your fans will realize that you never really wanted to leave in the first place," Kate agreed. "Then life will be back to normal. Now that's worth celebrating!"

At just that moment, a string of fireworks went *Crack! Crack! Crack!* in the distance.

"Oh, that's right!" Sydney exclaimed. "It's the Fourth of July! Yankee Doodle Dandy!"

Kate looked in the distance as she heard more cracks. "I love fireworks. *Love* them! They always make me so happy!"

"I still say they're lighting fireworks just for you," her mother said, reaching to hug her. "It's a nationwide celebration for my girl!"

"Just like every year on your birthday," her dad added.

"I wish I'd been born on the Fourth of July," Sydney said with a sigh. "Must be nice to have such a huge deal made over your birthday."

They all laughed.

"Well, if you're in the mood for celebrating, it's a good thing we don't have a game tonight," Mr. Smith said. "Would you all like to be my guests for a Fourth of July pool party here? And then front-row seats as I emcee for one of the largest fireworks displays in the nation?"

"You mean a Kate Oliver *birthday* party," Kate said with a giggle.

"That, too," Mrs. Smith said and winked.

"In that case, we'd love to!" Kate looked at her mother and father. "Is it okay? I only have a few more days before Sydney has to go back home, and I want to make the best of them. Please, please, please!"

"No begging necessary!" her father said. "I'd love to. I've been wanting to get to know our new friends better, anyway."

The Olivers got their swimsuits from home and then the families spent the rest of the evening together, cooking hamburgers and hot dogs on the outside grill and talking about how God had turned their situation around. Kate had a great time laughing and talking. . .and best of all, there were no bad guys to think about!

At the end of the evening, after all of the fireworks had lit up the skies, the Olivers climbed into the van to go home. As they drove, Kate asked her father a question. "What's going to happen to SWAT-bot now, Dad? The police aren't going to keep him, are they?"

"Only long enough to retrieve the information from his hard drive," her father explained. "The photos and the audio/video recording should help them prove their case against James Kenner. Well, that, and his fingerprints all over SWAT-bot."

"I'm so proud of you, Dad," Kate said, reaching to give him a hug. "If you hadn't created that little robot, the police never would have caught the bad guy."

"Aw, thanks, honey. But I was just thinking about how proud I am of *you*. You did a great job following all of the clues!"

"She's certainly a chip off the old block," Kate's mother said.

Chip off the old block? Kate wanted to ask what that meant, but Sydney interrupted her.

"When we get back to your house, don't you think we should e-mail the other Camp Club Girls and tell them what happened?"

"What time is it?" Kate asked.

"Ten fifteen," her mother said. "And it's okay to use the computer—but not for long, okay? I know how eager you girls are to share your news."

"Thanks, Mom! I can't wait to thank my friends for their help!" Kate said. "If they hadn't worked so hard to get people to our blog site, we never would have figured out the whole PhilliesFan29 thing."

When they arrived home, the girls signed onto the Internet and went straight to the Camp Club Girls chat room. They found Bailey and McKenzie already in the chat room. Kate quickly filled them in with information about James Kenner's arrest.

Bailey: *I'll text the other CCG and tell them it's*

solved, if that's okay with you, Birthday Girl.
Kate: *Of course! And I'll e-mail them with details tomorrow.*

When Kate dressed for bed, Sydney was already curled up under the covers, fast asleep. Kate slipped into the spot beside her and prayed, *Thank You, Lord, for watching over us as we solved this case. I'm so grateful that You led me to James Kenner. Lord, I pray that You will help turn things around for Tony Smith and his family. Oh, and Lord. . .*

Just then, her cell phone rang. Kate looked at the caller ID and whispered, "I'll be right back, Lord. Better get that!"

She answered right away. "What's up, Andrew?"

"I just thought you would want to know. . .James Kenner confessed to the police. He's definitely the one who's been framing my dad."

"Did he say why?" Kate asked.

"Yes. Turns out, his younger brother is a shortstop who played college ball. He was supposed to get drafted to the pros this year. And he had his heart set on the Phillies."

"But there aren't any openings for that spot, right?" Kate asked. "Is that it?"

"Yes. I guess this James Kenner guy thought he was doing his brother a favor. If he could get my dad to leave the team—drive him away with these ugly rumors—then the Phillies would need a new shortstop."

"Oh, I see," Kate said. "He thought they would pick his brother to play in your dad's place."

"I guess." Andrew sighed. "It really makes me mad, Kate. I'm having a lot of trouble not being angry at James Kenner right now. I know I'm going to have to forgive him, but it might not be easy."

"Oh, I understand. Trust me," Kate said. "But just remember. . .the Bible says not to let the sun go down on your anger. It's never good to carry a grudge. But don't worry—Kenner will pay for this crime for a long time."

"I know." Andrew paused and then added, "Kate, thank you for all of your help. It's because of you that—"

"No, not me!" Kate interrupted him. "God is the One who solved all of this. And He's a far better supersleuth than I am. He's the best, in fact!"

"You're right!" Andrew agreed.

Kate looked over at Sydney, who slept soundly on the other side of the bed. "I guess I'd better go now, Andrew. I don't want to wake up Sydney."

"I'm awake," Sydney said with a groan.

Kate giggled as she whispered into the phone, "I'll talk to you later. Right now I'd better get some rest. I only have two more days with my friend, and I want to enjoy every minute!"

Words Have Power

On the morning after her birthday, Kate awoke before anyone else in the house. She spent several minutes lying in bed, praying silently. She didn't want to wake Sydney, after all.

Slipping quietly out of bed, she tiptoed down the stairs. Biscuit followed her, whimpering.

"I know!" she whispered. "You need to go outside!"

After letting Biscuit out, she got on the computer, excited about a brand-new idea. She signed onto the Internet and immediately started composing an e-mail to send to the Camp Club Girls, filling them all in.

Kate lost all track of time, but when she heard footsteps coming down the stairs, she glanced at the clock. Had she really been working more than an hour? Wow! The time had flown by!

Sydney sat down next to her, rubbing her eyes. "So what are you working on?" She yawned.

"Letting the CCG know what happened," Kate explained.

Sydney nodded. "It mainly happened because of you, Inspector Gadget! You're loaded with great ideas!"

Kate grabbed her necklace and held it between her fingertips with a smile. It felt good to have her friend's love and support, but it felt even better to know she'd helped track down the man who was hurting Tony Smith with his words!

Minutes later, everyone in the house awoke and came downstairs for breakfast. As Kate took a bite of her cereal, the phone rang. Her mother answered it. After a few minutes of talking, she hung up and came over to the girls with a surprised look on her face.

"It's Tony Smith," she said. "He wants to come over to talk to you two. Better hurry up and get dressed for the day! I'll tidy up the kitchen before he gets here."

Kate and Sydney scrambled from their seats and raced up the stairs.

"What do you think he wants to tell us?" Sydney asked. "I'm so curious!"

"I don't know." Kate shook her head. "But remember. . .he said he was going to surprise us with something special if we solved the case. Maybe we're about to find out what he meant by that! I can hardly wait!"

"Oh, that's right. I wonder what he's decided to do!" Sydney clasped her hands together. "It's going to be great, whatever it is!"

Kate slipped into a pair of jean shorts and grabbed her new Phillies shirt.

"There's another game tomorrow night," Kate said. "I wonder if we'll get to go."

"Oh, maybe *that's* the surprise!" Sydney said. "Maybe Tony Smith will give us tickets for one last game!"

The doorbell rang and they raced to answer the door. Mr. Smith stood there with Andrew. Kate invited them into the house. Tony greeted her parents and then turned to the girls with a broad smile.

"Remember I told you I had a special surprise for you if you solved the case?" he said.

"Of course!" Kate practically squealed.

Sydney looked at him with anticipation in her eyes. "Please tell us!"

"Yes, please tell us!" Kate echoed.

"Well. . ." He smiled, obviously trying to tease them a little. "One of you will get to toss the first pitch at tomorrow night's Phillies game."

"W–what?" Kate asked. Did he really say what she thought he had said?

"N–no way!" Sydney stammered.

Tony nodded. "You get to choose! So who's it gonna be?"

"Oh!" Kate could hardly breathe. The very idea of going onto that field in front of millions and zillions of people gave her the shivers. Why would anyone want to do such a scary thing? She'd rather solve a hundred thousand crimes before doing that!

Out of the corner of her eye, she saw Sydney. Her friend's eyes were wide and she looked like she might cry.

"I. . .I. . .I. . ." Sydney stared at Tony, her mouth wide open.

Kate laughed, realizing what she needed to say. "Sydney, it *has* to be you. I wouldn't begin to know how to throw a baseball. I'd be embarrassed to even try."

"A—are you s—sure?" Sydney stammered. "Really? Me?"

"Really!" Kate, Andrew, and Mr. Smith said in unison.

"I get to toss the first ball?" Sydney began to squeal at the top of her lungs—so loud that Kate and everyone else put their fingers in their ears. "Oh, I don't believe it!" she shouted. "I don't! I'm going to put this on my résumé. My sports résumé, I mean. Can you believe it? Me! Sydney Lincoln—tossing the opening pitch at a Phillies game. Oh, Mr. Smith, how can I ever thank you? What can I ever do? Write more articles? Tell people what a great player you are? Start a fan club?"

He laughed. "No, Sydney. You've already done so much for me. Andrew told me about the Camp Club Girls. Between your work and your prayers, you guys saved my career. So you owe me nothing for this. I'm just happy that you're happy."

"Happy!" Sydney's eyes filled with tears. "Next to being

in the Junior Olympics, this is the greatest thing that's ever happened to me."

She kept talking about what a wonderful experience this was going to be, but Kate hardly heard a word. She was far too excited just watching Sydney's face, and she could hardly wait to tell the other Camp Club Girls!

"Oh, speaking of great things. . ." Kate snapped her fingers as another of her brilliant beyond brilliant ideas occurred. "Mr. Smith. . ."

"Tony," he said with a grin.

"Tony, can you stay a few more minutes? My dad and I have something in the basement we need to show you."

She looked at her father for support, and he nodded as he said, "I think the timing is finally right."

"Sounds like a mystery," Tony said. "But I'm happy to take a look. I'm curious." He followed as they all clambered down the stairs and into the basement. Kate turned on the light and Tony looked around in wonder. "You have a lot of really cool things down here," he said.

"Thanks," Kate and her dad said in unison.

"But there's one thing we really have to show you," Kate explained. She reached for the Robo-Brace. "It's something my dad and I have been working on. . .together."

Tony looked at it curiously. "What's this, Kate?"

"Well, it's for children with muscular dystrophy. To help them move their arms and hands. We call it Robo-Brace."

His eyes grew wide with excitement. "Really? Show me how it works."

She did just that and Biscuit began to jump up and down, trying to get in on the fun. He went *Yap, yap, yap!* as she moved her arms this way and that way.

Tony watched with an expression of awe. "That's the most amazing thing I've ever seen. And now that the Muscular Dystrophy Foundation has asked me to continue working as a spokesperson, I'm in a great position to help you get the news out on this."

"I'm hoping to get it patented soon," Kate's dad explained.

"I'm sure you will!" Tony nodded. "It's going to help so many people!"

"I'm so glad everyone has figured out what a great guy my dad is," Andrew said. "It was really hard to hear the mean things people were saying, especially when I knew none of them were true! That James Kenner needs to go to jail for a long, long time!"

"God will handle all of that," Tony said. "I've already prayed and forgiven James Kenner. What he did was wrong, but I have to forgive him anyway."

Kate sighed. What a good man Tony Smith was! And now everyone would know it!

They all spent a little more time looking at Robo-Brace and some of her father's other inventions, and then the adults went back upstairs to have some coffee. That left Kate, Sydney, and Andrew in the basement alone.

"I really wonder why James Kenner decided to use such a mean way to pick on your dad," Sydney said. "Those rumors he started could've ruined his career."

"I know," Andrew said. "But the police explained it to us. James Kenner said that rumors were what ruined his brother's chances to get in the pros, and he wanted the same thing to happen to the man who took his place."

"Wow! See what happens when rumors get started?" Kate said. She paused a moment then thought of something. "Oh! Our rumor box! It's still upstairs with those two rumors in it. What do we do with it?"

"Hmm." Andrew shook his head. "I don't know."

"Well, all of that stuff about Tony not liking to play for the Phillies was definitely a rumor," Sydney said. "So it can stay in the box. But I think I'd better take out the one about Kate Oliver being the smartest girl in the world—especially now! That's no rumor. It's the truth!"

Kate laughed. "Trust me, that one's not true either. I'm sure there are millions of smarter people than me. But as long as we're starting good rumors, how about I start one about you?"

"Me?" Sydney shrugged. "What sort of rumor?"

"Well. . ." Kate thought about it for a minute. "I think you know more about sports than any other girl. And even though you always try to win whatever game you're playing, you're always nice to others. You play fair. And you work hard to be the best you can be!"

"That's not a rumor either." Andrew laughed. "That's just the plain, simple truth."

Kate thought about that for a moment. "I guess you're right. Maybe we don't need a rumor box at all. Maybe God just wants to remind us to be really careful every time we hear someone say something about someone else—careful to make sure it's the truth before we spread it around to others."

"Exactly!" Sydney said.

"And we also have to remember that our words have power," Kate said thoughtfully. "Whether it's a rumor. . .or mean words or even nice words. Our words make a difference to others."

"The Bible says the power of life and death is in the tongue," Sydney said. "I read that just last week. Our words will either build others up or tear them down."

"Well, I'm going to be a builder-upper, then!" Kate said with a smile. "I'm gonna watch every word that comes out of my mouth so that others won't be hurt."

Sydney nodded. "I'm going to do the same. And we can send an e-mail to Bailey and McKenzie and the others to let them know we're going to be a rumor-free group!"

"Ooh! Maybe we should print up some T-shirts!" Kate

said. "They could say 'YOU AND ME, RUMOR FREE'!"

Sydney laughed. "Great idea!"

As they made their way up the stairs to join the adults, all three chanted in unison, "Rumor Free! You and Me!"

CHAPTER 16

Supersleuths Forever!

On the morning after Sydney tossed the opening pitch at the Phillies game, Kate's mother drove the girls to the train station. All along the way they laughed and talked, reliving all of the fun they'd had over the past two weeks. Kate could hardly believe so much had happened. . .and in such a short time. It felt like months had flown by, not weeks!

"Remember when you thought bases were place mats?" Sydney asked.

"Yes." Kate gave her a sheepish grin.

"And you thought the field was a court?" Sydney continued.

"I remember, I remember." Kate groaned, feeling more embarrassed than ever. "I'll be the first to admit, I didn't know anything about baseball back then."

"But you sure do now! And you were a lot of fun at last night's game. You even cheered in the right places!" Sydney said. After a pause, she gave Kate a funny look and asked, "So. . .do you like it?"

"*Like* it? Like what?" Kate asked.

"Like *baseball*!" Sydney laughed. "Are you starting to like the game?"

"Are you kidding?" Kate giggled. "I'm already thinking of an article I can add to our Phillies site. I'm going to keep it going, you know. And the Camp Club Girls will help." Her heart swelled with excitement. "I can't believe I actually like a sport." She laughed. "How funny is that?"

"Pretty funny!" her mother said from the front seat. "But it might interest you to know that I played tennis in college."

"What?" Kate sat straight up in her seat. "Why didn't you ever tell me about that?"

"Oh, I don't know," her mother said with a shrug. "Just never came up, I guess. I was also on the swim team in high school. I've always enjoyed sports."

"Well, go figure!" Kate said. "The apple *doesn't* fall far from the tree." She got tickled by that statement and started laughing. Before long, she and Sydney were all giggles. . .until they arrived at the train station. Then their laughter quickly turned to sadness.

"I can't believe you have to go back home," Kate said, giving her friend a hug. "I don't want you to leave! I'm going to miss you so much!"

"I know," Sydney agreed. "Me, too! But I need to get home to my mom. It's not easy on her, now that my dad's not there."

"I know." Kate gave her friend another hug. "Oh, but promise me we'll see each other again really soon. Promise?"

"Promise!" Sydney said, flashing a broad smile. "We're the Camp Club Girls, remember!"

"Supersleuths forever!" Kate shouted with glee.

"Supersleuths forever!" Sydney echoed.

She then looked at Kate with a twinkle in her eyes, and together they added one last line, just for fun! "Rumor Free! You and Me!"

If you enjoyed
KATE'S PHILADELPHIA FRENZY
be sure to read other
CAMP CLUB GIRLS
books from BARBOUR PUBLISHING

Book 1: Mystery at Discovery Lake
ISBN 978-1-60260-267-0

Book 2: Sydney's DC Discovery
ISBN 978-1-60260-268-7

Book 3: McKenzie's Montana Mystery
ISBN 978-1-60260-269-4

Book 4: Alexis and the
Sacramento Surprise
ISBN 978-1-60260-270-0

Book 6: Bailey's Peoria
Problem
ISBN 978-1-60260-272-4

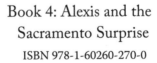

AVAILABLE WHEREVER BOOKS ARE SOLD.